# Tales from Floor Fifty-Four

## Volume One

**By Ryan Hunt**

*Floor Fifty-Four Publishing*

*www.floorfiftyfour.co.uk*

*First released by Floor Fifty-Four Publishing 2021*



*ISBN: 978-1-7398228-1-1*



*Cover artwork by Diletta De Santis*
*(https://www.artstation.com/didies)*

*Floor Fifty-Four Logo Design by Amy Gooding*
*Floor Fifty-Four Website by Oliver Cox*

*This first book is for all the writers I met along the way. It's not easy. There were so many creative worlds that I was lucky to glimpse, and may never become real. This book is also for my brother, Joel, who proofread every story, and never stops being my creative jousting partner. 'Abigail' was his idea. It won't be his last contribution to the Floor.*

# Contents

51

52

53

# 54

*Every nation has one.*
*A pit to hide their secrets.*
*The once-great British Empire still holds the largest known to man. Fifty-Four floors deep, filled with mysteries, horrors and lies. Within this tomb lurk secrets too strange for our world to know.*

*A thousand objects, creatures and artifacts are tucked away on Floor Fifty-Four, each unique. Imprisoned in transparent cages, they will sit forever. Studied. Guarded. Contained.*

*Every item has a story. Every item had to be captured and dragged down to these depths, often against its will.*

*It was once said the sun never set on the British Empire. Perhaps that was because they knew what lurked in the shadows...*

# Item 001

Secrets can be funny old things. Wriggling. Squirming. Desperate to be free. Most secrets are fragile; always on the brink of shattering. A single misplaced word, even a too-long pause, causes spiderweb splinters across their surface, like heavy boots upon a frozen lake. Some secrets lay tucked away in tight-lipped corpses, taken to the grave, buried and forgotten. But the rarest kind of secrets - a curious few - are too strange to even exist.

Powerful authorities ensure they are removed from the world we know. Our everyday life cannot handle something so inexplicable. So horrific. So bizarre. For our safety and sanity, these particular secrets are scurried out of sight, thrown into a pit, and locked away.

Floor Fifty-Four is one such pit. If you were to step foot inside its sprawling halls, you would be forgiven for getting lost. It is a maze of twisting corridors, scientific laboratories and glass-fronted prison cells. Here, those curious secrets are put on full display. Observed. Studied. Restrained. Here, they are known as 'Items of Interest'. Eyeless horrors that seem to watch anyone walking past their cells. Here, there are hundreds of them. If you were of a curious mind, you could spend days exploring a single wing. Careless minds might never return.

Most cells are the same. Cold, silent rooms containing a single object within. Harsh artificial light illuminates it. Surveillance cameras watch it. Guards patrol outside. If left alone, these items might stay as ordinary as they appear.

But there is danger here. The most deadly items usually

have unique rooms. They require a specific containment procedure. No expense spared, because the alternative is too terrible to consider. A small poison ivy plant, surrounded by walls and flooring made of terracotta pottery, napalm poised to flood the chamber at a moment's notice. A house cat made of black and white static, with everything he needs to make him stay. And then there is The Narrator.

His cell was never cold, for a start. A roaring fireplace sat at its centre, flames flickering to life whenever the temperature dropped too low. Gilded artwork adorned the walls; printed copies of famous masterpieces that can be changed upon request. A wall clock, pendulum swinging, faintly ticking as it counted the passing time. Embossed black wallpaper, hanging gas lamps and an intricately-patterned Persian rug. Most noticeably of all, unlike all the others, his cell had a distinct absence of reinforced glass. A heavy, black door was the only way in or out. No, this room was not like the others in the slightest.

Painted on the oak floor boards, a thick red line ran in a tight perimeter around the remaining contents of the room. A book shelf, a red leather armchair, and a man who was not a man at all.

Wrapped in a checkered three-piece suit, his clothes very much looked a part of him. As did the chair. As did the books. He adjusted his half moon glasses before pulling himself away from the page he was reading.

"Ahh," he smiled, snapping the book shut. "You're here at last."

From the black door drifted a soft beeping melody, and with a sharp hiss the door began to swing inward on its hinges. Sterile light flooded into the room, and the opening door revealed several figures lingering in a particularly-cold-looking concrete corridor. The first cautiously made her way inside. She was draped in a long, white overcoat and clutched a metal tray in her quivering hands. Atop the tray was a china cup, filled with tea, and a matching china plate with three biscuits sliding across its smooth surface. She crept forwards, eyes wide. Behind her, equally as watchful, were two burly guards, clad in rippling black armour and clutching pronged weapons which sparked and sizzled the air around them.

The strange man smiled warmly, and removed his glasses. "Not them. Though their appearance is a timely one. Thank you, dear."

The tray was offered to the strange man with outstretched hands, shaking so violently that the plate and cup rattled against the metal, threatening to spill the tea entirely. As slow as a snake, the man reached out and took the tray, snapping the rattle to a sudden halt. The woman flinched, emitting a small squeak as her legs took an involuntary, instinctual step backwards.

"It's a good job she didn't overfill the cup," said the man, his smile nowhere to be seen. "My tea would have slopped over the sides."

Hands raised defensively, her entire body still trembling, the woman fled the room, darting between her two guards with rabbit-quick footsteps. They too left the room, not turning their backs, stepping together. Another melodic beep, another hiss, and the black door swivelled shut, hiding the three figures and the cold corridor once more.

The strange man set down the tray on the oak table beside him. His smile returned, warm as fresh apple crumble, and he stared intently at the air before him.

"No, I wasn't talking to them. I was talking to you."

His smile deepened, head tilting ever so slightly.

"That's right. You. Reading this book."

His attention turned to the metal tray, and he snatched up the china cup by the handle. His fingers danced in the air, hovering above the biscuits, deciding which to grasp.

"It feels like I've been waiting forever," he announced, selecting the middle biscuit; a chocolate digestive. "But you know what they say about good things and waiting..."

Blowing hot steam away from his cup of tea, he took a delicate first sip. If it was scalding hot, he showed no signs. Instead, he set the cup back down and took a first bite of his biscuit, before returning that to its plate too. Small tastes were enough for this man, it seemed.

His eyes drifted to the bookcase, and he stretched in his chair to reach. His fingers tapped the spine of each book in turn. "But where to start...? Hmm..." Leaning completely over the armrest, he never left his seat, his fingers stalking the shelves. After a moment, he settled on the furthest book, snatching it up. "Aah. Yes. At the beginning."

"At this..." he paused, gesturing to the room around himself, "wonderful place. Floor Fifty-Four."

"As long as there have been people, there have been stories. Myths. Legends. Tales to tell around campfires, after darkness digs its claws into the world. Stories that have spread from generation to generation, to you. Some small part of you, deep down in your bones must have wondered. Could they all... just be stories? Fantasy? Fiction? Some, of course, are entirely conjured from wild imaginations. But all of them? Every story? Ever?"

The man who was not a man chuckled to himself. A quiet, rasping sound.

"Magic. Monsters. Gods. They were all real. For a time.

Before your ancestors turned the tables. Before those secrets were locked away, the keys swallowed. But, just as a dirty little secret eventually wriggles and squirms its way free, so too, do remnants of the old world ripple in the shadows of the new. There's a reason you fear the dark. A reason all people have shared fears, seared into the very edges of their minds."

His smile widened. And widened. And widened. Alone in his cell, the strange man stared intently at nothing in particular, his eyes sliding in and out of focus. He continued to stretch his smile, until it became too wide for his face. Until his lips sounded like tightening leather straps.

"This place," he said, smile vanishing as he gestured to the room around him, "is where such things get locked away. The Ministry of Secrets. Fifty-four floors of horrors and lies. And this... this is the bottom rung of the ladder. Floor Fifty-Four."

"I suppose you could see for yourself. I mean, it's right outside. If I simply nudge your perspective a little, just beyond these walls, you could roam freely. You'd have to put up with their chattering though. Dull questions, with dull answers. Go ahead, I'll wait."

He made a dismissive shooing gesture whilst opening the hardcover of the book in his hands, before licking his finger and turning the page.

***

In the corridors of Floor Fifty-Four, Dr Suzie Milton walked unsteadily on black kitten heels. It wasn't the shoes that were making her legs wobble, though. She had been warned that Item 001 could be unnerving. She had been told it might talk to her, and that under no circumstances was she to cross the red line. But seeing 'The Narrator' in the flesh was still making her fingers tremble, and she hadn't yet been able to shake loose an unsettling feeling that had nestled between the bones of her spine.

"...every day?" she asked the two guards walking alongside her. "Someone brings that... thing... a cup of tea every day?"

"And biscuits," Bryce added in a smug growl. "Trust me, you don't want to forget the biscuits."

He was enjoying this. Bryce always seemed to enjoy himself when Suzie was afraid. He liked to drag it out, to bathe in it, like a water buffalo. Maybe seeing others scared made him feel less afraid himself. Or maybe he was just an arse.

They walked past row after row of glass-fronted cells. Each cell had nothing inside except one item. Some were strange. Some were mundane. But Suzie knew by now that if she didn't immediately recognise an item, it was best to ignore it entirely. At least she knew what most of them did now. Most of the ones on display, at least. As they reached the angel statue - it wasn't crying today - Suzie turned away from the guards and started to make her excuses.

"I'd better go and speak to Dr Auburn. There was nothing in the report about it speaking like that."

"Aah, it talks all the time," said Bryce, waving his hand. "Loves to talk, that one."

"It's shutting him up that's the problem," said Phil, and when Bryce wasn't looking, he subtly nodded his head towards the other guard. Apparently he wasn't just talking about Item 001. Suzie shared a small smile with the old man, but work was still at the forefront of her mind.

"It talks to people who enter, yes," Suzie agreed. "Tries to lure them into conversation, but... didn't you feel as though it wasn't talking to us?"

"I just ignore it, to be honest," said Bryce, casually tapping his armoured plating with his baton.

"'Not them'," Suzie muttered, mulling it over and over. "That was the first thing it said. Almost as if it were already mid-conversation..."

Bryce shook his head and turned to the other guard. "I hate it when they do this," he announced, as if Suzie wasn't standing directly behind him. "You can see the wheels turning and you just know we're gonna end up pulling double shifts."

"I think Dr Milton's right," admitted Phil, "Normally it says my name, asks me how many days 'til retirement. I never know, but it does. Tells me exactly how many days, then it laughs. Barely noticed us today. Seemed almost bored by us."

Bryce's expression soured a little, but only for a moment. As he whirled around to face Suzie, his eyes glittered with amusement. "Always forget you're a doctor," he said with a smirk. His gaze swept her up and down, lingering on all the places she wished he wouldn't. "Doctor's are usually... bigger."

Suzie felt her face glow ember-hot. She wanted to storm off, or better yet - say something! - to show Bryce that his actions were hurtful and intolerable, but her mouth wouldn't make any noise, and her feet... her feet were far too polite. Far too timid. The most confrontation she could muster was looking at the floor. Even that felt rude.

"Well, you heard Dr Milton, she's got places to be," Phil said after a moment, and he turned away.

Bryce didn't follow. Instead he leaned forwards and lowered his voice to a growl. "Well I'd hardly be a gentleman if

I let the lady walk alone..."

With that, he started walking, and Suzie's too-polite feet followed. Eager to talk about something - anything - instead of letting Bryce grapple his arms around the conversation, Suzie returned to Item 001.

"In the report, it says sometimes the cell is empty. Sometimes Item 001 just... leaves?"

Bryce made a show of rolling his eyes. "Call it 'The Narrator', will ya? We don't all speak numbers."

"Well, it's just that nicknames create attachments and a false sense of..." Suzie glanced at Bryce's grim face and sighed. "Fine... 'The Narrator'... sometimes leaves its cell. Isn't that a little concerning?"

Bryce shrugged. "He always comes back."

"But that's not the point," said Suzie in an exasperated voice, "how does he escape? Where does he go? And if he can leave whenever he wants, why does he come back?"

They walked between glass fronted cells, ignoring the items within. In fact, they were so engaged in their conversation, they didn't even seem to notice the man sat in a red leather armchair, just a few paces ahead. He didn't pay them any attention either, nose buried in his book, legs lazily sprawled out into the corridor. Though each step brought them closer to colliding, neither party seemed aware of the other.

As Dr Milton and Bryce walked close enough to touch, the man tucked in his legs at the last possible moment. Both the burly guard and the diminutive scientist carried on down the corridor, completely oblivious to their close encounter.

The Narrator looked up from his book, holding his place with a finger. Once more he looked into empty space and spoke, arching a wry eyebrow as he did so.

"I did warn you. So terribly dull. Dreary questions from dreary people. Not that they don't each have their moments, mind you..." his eyes drifted away, wandering towards his vast shelf of books. He seemed to catch himself, and smiled. "Another time, perhaps."

In the distance, the two figures turned a corner and disappeared. The Narrator didn't spare them a glance, but he flashed a wicked grin. "You're wondering why they couldn't see me."

Resuming his place amongst the pages, the man stroked gently down the page. "I've often found that words possess a certain magic. Place them in a specific order and they can become something else entirely. A portal to another world. Another time. Another place. Why, the right words in the right sequence could make someone fall in love with you, or try to kill you. And if a mere sentence can hold magic, imagine the power of an entire book. Skip ahead, and you could read the future. Flick back a few pages and..."

As he spoke, he did so, leafing through the book in his hands. Dr Milton and Bryce were once more in the corridor, approaching him and unaware. Mid-conversation, they spoke the same words they had just moments before. This time, however, The Narrator left a single leg stretched out from his chair. As Bryce walked past, his boot clipped the barest slither of trouser, and he stumbled.

Muttering a curse, Bryce turned around to face The Narrator, but saw nothing except an empty corridor. Muttering about the uneven floor, Bryce resumed his conversation and walked away.

"Forwards, backwards. It's as simple as turning a page." The Narrator pursed his lips and traced the words in the page with a finger. He lingered on this very sentence, a sentence that described him in the corridor. The words changed. And he wasn't in the corridor any more. Sat on his red leather chair, he wiped dust from the glass of the cell he had placed himself inside. Outside, just beyond the glass, Dr Milton and Bryce walked past, repeating their conversation once more.

"Change a few words," said The Narrator, "and I can be here, instead of there. And if the story gets tiresome..."

He turned his head to his vast bookcase, which had followed him inside the cell. Still at the same angle. Still the same distance away. As his eyes drifted among the spines, their colours shifted, their titles flickered. Book swelled and shrank as pages came and went. The Narrator smiled. "There are always more."

He snapped his book shut, and was back in his room once more. The flames in his hearth roared at his appearance, and he took a sip of tea. Thirst apparently quenched, he set it down and turned back to address the air.

"So yes, in a manner of speaking, I can go to any place, visit any time. I can watch from the shadows, or if I truly want to... I can make myself known. But doing that too much that would change the story. Ruin it."

The Narrator straightened his back and adjusted himself, settling into his chair. "And you didn't come here for bad stories now, did you?"

He shook the book in his hands. "This. This is what you came for. An introduction. A curious toe, dangled into unknown waters, so to speak."

Without looking, he collected his cup of tea and clutched it close to him.

"So. Let's get the taste on your tongue. There are hundreds of items just outside these very walls. Now they are simply prisoners, half understood and locked tightly away from prying eyes, but once there was a time where they roamed free. Before they found themselves in this... zoo. This museum. This prison for the strange. Someone had to find them, after all. Some poor, unassuming soul whose thread became entangled and, so often, cut short."

The Narrator reached to his shelf, and scooped up a blackened book. Smoke drifted from within, and the Narrator seemed to ignore the still-glowing embers around its scorched edges.

"Which does make me think of a story..."

# "The Reverse Voodoo Doll"

*[retrieved from victim's diary following incident]*

Most people have a relic from their childhood they keep around. Maybe it's a beloved toy they can't bring themselves to throw away. Perhaps a photo of a captured moment; a happy memory to keep in their wallet. Maybe it's a scar, from the time they fell whilst doing something beyond their ability, or worse - the scars that can't be seen, the ones that hide on the inside. Baggage that has moulded who they are. Quirks. Passions. Fears.

We all have something we keep. Mine is a dark wooden box. I hate that fucking box. I hide it away, stuffed at the back of my bottom drawer, wrapped in a tea towel so I don't even have to look at it. My husband doesn't know why I refused to have 'walnut' laminate flooring in our dining room. It's because it reminds me of that bloody box.

Well, today he found it, and I don't know what to do. I freaked out. There are a million ways I could have handled it better, but I panicked, I saw the wood, saw him reach for the clasp. I actually scratched his arm pretty badly without meaning to. I've managed to convince him just to drop it for now, but I know he thinks I'm crazy. And, worst of all, I know that the moment I leave this house, he's going to try and find it, and look inside. And then what?

I suppose I should explain.

Growing up in the eighties wasn't easy, not for my brother and me at least. To this day, I still don't know for sure what my mother did for work (though I have my suspicions). What I do know is that we were as close to poverty as it's possible to get without moving outdoors, or out of mainland Europe. Most people dismiss Liverpool because of the 'funny accent', but it has darker shadows than anywhere I've ever been in my life. There's a story about a man who travelled the world on his bicycle; visited every country then returned to England, only to get his bike nicked in Liverpool. That says it all. Just like any city, it's got its nice parts, then there's the underbelly, where the scrotes live.

Well we were the scrotes. Me, my big brother Jacob and our occasional mother - who visited us from time to time to sleep and eat. Looking back, it was a lot like having a cat. She'd come when she wanted something, leave whenever she liked, and occasionally bring us gifts we didn't appreciate or want. Cats bring dead birds. My mother bought gold watches, cigarettes and pot noodles. I was seven years old and I loved her so very, very much.

With no father and an infrequent mother, Jacob had no choice but to become the man of the house. I say house. It was a one room bedsit, with a mattress on the floor. Jacob was twelve years old, and whilst he always seemed like a giant to me, he was too young and scrawny to mix with the bigger kids on the block, especially with a younger sister in tow. So we stayed in the flat most of the time, garnering annoyance and sympathy in equal measures. Our flat was four stories high, and filled with all sorts of wonderful characters you'd cross the street to avoid. There were bad ones, like the old man we only ever knew as 'Mr Creepy'. There were good ones, like Mrs Cooper, who would give us food whenever we passed her door.

But my absolute favourite was a rather large Jamaican lady who called herself Mama Jane.

She had an accent that was thick as treacle, and owned the shop at the bottom of our flat. Mama Jane's shop was the kind of bric-a-brac weirdo-museum you just don't see on the highstreet anymore, and since she didn't mind our company, it became our adoptive home. Whilst the shop sold any type of item you can imagine, Mama Jane had a particular fascination with dolls. If it was miniature and had anything vaguely resembling a face, Mama Jane would buy it, display it in her shop window and pronounce it was "not fah sale". Even those racist little Golly-Dollies that people used to collect. Sometimes people told her she shouldn't put them in her shop window, but she just shrugged and said it was her shop, and if people didn't like it they could stick it where the sun don't shine. "Nothing with a smile like that can be hateful," she'd say.

If we helped around the shop, we could play with any toy we liked, but only one. I don't really know how much we helped, but Mama Jane would let us play with something from her shop almost every day. There was an unspoken code about it, something of a ritual. We wouldn't pick anything that looked like it would break, and Mama Jane would let us stay in the shop for as long as we liked, providing we didn't bother customers. This was an easy rule to follow, as they were practically none existent.

People did bring things to Mama Jane though, and one particular day a tall Jamaican man with dreadlocks dangling over his shoulder brought a walnut coloured box into the shop. I knew he was Jamaican, because whenever someone from Jamaica came into the shop, Mama Jane's accent would intensify to the point where a seven year old Liverpudlian girl could no longer gain any meaning. I was playing with my favourite vintage doll - a horrific sun bleached thing that I called Tabitha - and Jacob was playing with his train, driving it along the stained carpet enthusiastically.

"Watch the shop, children," Mama Jane called behind her as she and the man disappeared into the back to talk business.

After a while, they came back, talking quietly amongst themselves. I could tell Mama Jane was excited. The man's box was gone, and as he left the shop, Mama Jane locked the door, turned the 'open' sign to 'closed' then burst into gleeful laughter, stomping her feet and swaying from side to side.

"What you get today Mama?" Jacob asked.

"Oh child," she said, clapping her hands together, "come see!"

We both placed our toys back carefully on their respective shelves - abandoning a toy meant you did not want it, Mama always claimed - then followed her into the back of the shop. This in itself was something of a rare treat, and her excitement was infectious, even without me or Jacob knowing what exactly we were excited about. Inside her back office, on her desk was the dark wooden box. Now I could see it properly. About the size of two big books, stacked on top of each other, it was locked tight with two brass clasps. Mama Jane brushed her hand along the walnut lid and looked down at us.

"D'ya believe in magic, children?" she asked in a whisper. Her wide eyes made me nod without even really thinking about the question.

"Magic's for kids," said Jacob defiantly.

"Hmm, that what you think, is it?" said Mama, her voice purring. She snapped one clasp open, then the other. Pausing with her hand on the lid, she met our eyes and drank us in. I realised I was leaning so far forwards, I was close to toppling on my face.

Whatever Mama was thinking, she decided to proceed, and lifted the lid. Jacob stood on tip toes to peer inside, but I was too short to see. All I could see was the green velvet interior of the case, and Mama Jane carefully lowered her hands inside the box. She was so tender lifting the contents out, at first I thought it was a newborn baby. As I got my first good look, I found myself disappointed. It was just a plain doll made out of a hessian sack. It had black button eyes and a stitched-on smile made from black thread. It didn't have hands, hair or any clothing. I couldn't see why Mama Jane was so excited about this boring doll until she placed it down. Rather than crumpling to the floor like every other doll I'd ever seen, it remained upright as Mama Jane took her hands away. Even though it was bent forwards, with its arms almost touching the carpet, it didn't fall over. Even my childlike grasp of physics told me this was strange, though I didn't understand why.

Then it began to move. It lifted its hessian arms and straightened, standing completely upright. When it clapped its little stumps together, Mama Jane started laughing in her great, big, booming way that meant something was truly delighting her.

We'd seen puppets before, but they had strings. It was a game that we chose to play along with. This was something else. This was real magic.

I was so enraptured with the moving doll, it took me a long time to notice that Mama Jane was clapping in time with it. When each of its hessian hands joined together, a clap would sound from above me. At first I thought she was copying it, but then as I glanced from one to the other, I realised it was the other way around. The doll was copying Mama Jane's movements. Perfectly. As though they were twins.

“What is it?” I asked.

“How does it work?” asked Jacob.

Mama Jane just laughed, and began walking around the room. The little doll did the same. As they moved, it almost looked like a syncronised dance routine. She jumped into the air, and the doll leapt off the floor in a mirror image, landing back on its feet with ease. We both applauded in sheer, childish glee.

“I want a go!” said Jacob.

Mama Jane leant over to him and wagged a finger. On the floor, the doll wiggled a stumpy limb. “It’s not so easy, child,” said Mama.

Jacob scrunched up his face, eyes locked on the doll. Mama Jane ruffled his hair and the doll reached into empty space to do the same.

“What’s its name?” I asked.

“He don’t have a name yet.”

That seemed a little sad to me. I waved at him and said “hello!”

To my surprise, the doll waved back. Mama did the same, waving in an identical fashion. Even though I knew Mama was controlling it, I was impressed how much it looked like the doll was truly waving at me. Its button eyes were staring right at me. Mama seemed less impressed though, and snatched up the doll, placed him inside the box and clasped it shut so quickly I almost didn’t believe it had happened. She rested over the box for quite a long time, long enough for me and Jacob to share a worried look. When Mama Jane turned around, she had stopped smiling, and her cheeks had gone pale.

“I don’t wancha to tell no one about this, ya hear?” she said.

We both nodded frantically. It wasn't like we had anyone to tell besides each other.

"Run along now," she said, scuttling us out of the back office. We said goodbye, but Mama Jane didn't say it back. The door to the office slammed shut behind us and was promptly locked.

Me and Jacob went upstairs, excitedly babbling to each other about the doll and what we would make it do when we had our turns. I began thinking of names for the doll, but Jacob didn't like any of my suggestions. Our real mother didn't come home that night, and I woke up a few times to Jacob accidentally jabbing me with a knee or elbow as he tossed and turned in the night. I remember opening my eyes to see him barely visible in the darkness, staring up at the ceiling.

"You ok?" I asked.

"I don't get how it works."

"Mama said it was magic," I replied, closing my eyes again.

"Magic's not real," Jacob said in a grumpy voice, throwing himself onto his side.

That night I dreamed of dancing dolls. Vintage Victorian ones, with rippling dresses. Barbies, all box-fresh and pretty. Golly dollies and cabbage patch kids. All holding hands in a huge circle and twirling, twirling, twirling. At the centre of it all, the hessian doll, with his button eyes and stitched-on smile.

I woke to Jacob nudging me, he already had his shoes on and he was shoving mine in my face.

"Come on," he said, leaping up and holding the door open for me.

Still rubbing sleep from my eyes, I started walking towards Mrs Cooper's flat, but Jacob pulled my arm and whirled me towards the staircase.

"But I'm hungry," I moaned, grabbing my belly dramatically.

"We'll get food later," said Jacob.

It was difficult to keep up with him that morning, he leapt downstairs and ran across the halls, stopping and waiting for me whenever he went too far. He grinned like a Cheshire Cat when the back door to Mama Jane's shop opened, and we crept inside. Mama was polishing shelves, and looked up at us as we entered.

"Good lord children, you out 'ere early today! I'm thinking you be wanting something?" She chuckled to herself and threw her duster over her shoulder.

"Have you got chores for us, Mama?" Jacob asked.

I watched him closely. We did chores, sure. But we never asked for them. Especially not Jacob. He was up to something. It didn't pass Mama Jane's notice either. She narrowed her eyes at us.

"Dat what ya both want, is it?"

I looked down at the floor, instinctually trying to look small and pitiful. "I want food," I said in a small voice.

She let out a disapproving 'hmm'. That was the sound she often made when we discussed our mother, either directly or indirectly. She held out her hand and led me through the back. As we walked away, she called to Jacob over her shoulder.

"Ya can clean the windows then boy! Keep gwan 'til ya see ya face in dem!"

Mama Jane didn't make us food very often, but I was hoping for a bit of lamb patty she'd shared with us once. No such luck on that day though; I just got jam on toast. She picked me up and let me sit on the counter of her makeshift kitchen, humming to herself as she buttered the toast and spread the jam. I told her of the names I'd thought for the doll, and she said they were pretty. After I'd eaten the last crust (Mama Jane would have never let us eat outside the kitchen) we walked back into the shop. I was ready to do some chores now, if it meant getting to play with the doll again. But as we walked around the shelves, the shop was empty. Where my brother should have been cleaning windows, there were just dingy net curtains and dolls perched on wooden chairs. Mama Jane walked outside, bell jangling as she looked left and right, but Jacob wasn't there. She came back inside, eyes darting around the shop. I tried looking too, but I couldn't see Jacob anywhere. My eyes fell on the door to the back office, which Mama Jane always kept locked.

Mama Jane seemed to have the same idea, and walked over to it, testing the handle. It opened. She pushed the door open and in the centre of the room was Jacob, scrambling on his knees. The walnut box was wide open, green velvet insides on show. Jacob was crying, and kept turning so we couldn't see what he had in his hands.

"I just wanted to see how it worked!" he said through tears.

He turned to us, and stuffing spilled out of his hands onto the floor. There was a small gash in the side of the doll, and Jacob's pocket knife lay on the floor, still open. I began crying too. Mama Jane moved over to Jacob, but as she moved, the doll stayed still. I charged towards Jacob and shoved him as hard as I could.

"You killed him!" I cried, eyes stinging so badly I couldn't even see my brother. "He didn't even have a name yet!"

Mama Jane said nothing, and as I wiped away my tears on a sleeve, I saw Jacob only had eyes for her, fearfully waiting for her reaction. We'd never seen Mama Jane angry, not really.

She was a woman who gave enough of a hint of what her anger could feel like, and that made you never want to prod further. In that moment, I became afraid too. Afraid that we'd lose our second home. Afraid that we'd lose Mama.

She plucked the doll from Jacob's hands and carried it over to her desk without saying a word. Mama calmly scooped up the stuffing pieces from the floor. The only sound was Jacob's choked sobs and my sniffles. Once every piece was on the table, she gazed down at the doll, shook her head and muttered something under her breath. Then she buried her head in her hands and said "this is a very bad thing you've done, Jacob."

It was the first time I'd ever heard her call either of us by name. We were always 'child' or 'children'. Mama Jane began to cry, and to our complete surprise, she turned and wrapped both of us into a tight hug.

"I'm really sorry Mama," whispered Jacob, "can you fix him?"

Still clutching one another, we walked over to the desk and stared at the unmoving doll. He looked so sad now, half deflated with his insides missing.

"I'm not sure I should Jacob," said Mama Jane, clamping hold of my arm and squeezing tight. "Some things in this world aren't to be toyed with."

Nodding to herself, Mama released us both and began to pull out the rest of the dolls stuffing. Once there was nothing left, she placed the doll back inside its walnut box and closed the lid. She placed it high on a bookshelf that even she could barely reach, and gathered up the stuffing into a pile.

"I'm sorry Mama," said Jacob again.

"Run along now, children," she said without looking at us.

We skulked out without another word, walked back up into the flats and spent the rest of the day sulking in our bedsit. Our own mother came home that night, quite late, collapsed without a word at the side of us onto the mattress. I waited until she fell asleep, then cuddled her arm.

Mornings with mother were terribly quiet. We would wait to see what mood she was in, creeping around and whispering. At the time, it just seemed like a game to me. I assumed we were being considerate, so as not to wake her. I realise now Jacob was doing it to extend the time we had where she wasn't awake.

The sirens ruined that. Police. Ambulance. More police. Something bad had happened, and our mother was convinced we should stay inside until they went away. Me and Jacob peeked through the curtains, watching the street below, but we couldn't see anything other than the tops of cars and people gawking at our building.

Eventually, anyone in uniform left, and our flat returned to normality. We could leave, and our mother was first to do so. Me and Jacob visited some neighbours, but kept inside the halls, too afraid to go back to Mama Jane's so soon. Mrs Cooper made us peanut butter sandwiches, and taught us how to tell the time. Or tried to, at least. We asked her what had happened with the police, but she said we didn't need to worry about that.

The next day, when we tried to visit Mama Jane, her door was locked and covered with tape. It said 'police' on it, but neither me or Jacob really knew what that meant. We went outside and tried to go to the front door, but that was locked too. It would be two more days before we found out Mama Jane was dead. Murdered, our mother said. Our neighbours had spared us all the gruesome details, but we pestered our mother until she spilled every last drop. Someone had stabbed her to death. They'd tried to make it look like suicide, but it was too obvious. They'd cut her open then put the knife in her hands.

I cried myself to sleep that night. Jacob refused to lie down, and curled up in a ball near the corner of the room. Our mother got sick of our whining and left in the middle of the night. She said Mama Jane was a bitch anyway, and probably got what was coming to her. I didn't believe that. I think that was the night any love for my mother began to unravel for me. She said a lot of nasty things that night. Things I don't truly remember, but I remember how it made me feel.

Days passed, and we began to hear more details. Mama Jane hadn't just been stabbed. She'd been disemboweled. Her intestines had been pulled all over the floor, and parts of them were missing.

When we heard that, we crept downstairs the same night, and Jacob showed me a trick with a pocket knife, a debit card and a door lock. I'd never been inside Mama Jane's shop in the darkness, and everything about it took on a dark tilt without her in the world. I clutched hold of Jacob as we made our way towards the office, where Jacob repeated his trick. Inside the room, I noticed the only thing different about the shop other than no light and no Mama. The carpet. A huge rectangle of carpet had been cut up and removed, just beneath the desk. At the time, it had baffled us. Now I know that was where she had died.

Of course, there was only one thing we wanted to check. One suspicion we couldn't let lie. Together we moved the chair and the desk, and Jacob climbed on top to reach the walnut box. As soon as he placed it down and ran his thumbs along the clasps, I wanted to leave. I wanted to forget the whole thing. I missed Mama and I couldn't bring her back. I was just a little girl, but I knew, I knew nothing good could come of this. But I couldn't stop Jacob. He snapped open the clasps and threw back the lid.

The doll was still inside. But it was whole again. The gash Jacob had made had been stitched back together. It's stuffing was back, apparently.

"Maybe Mama fixed it?" I hissed, creeping towards the door.

Jacob clearly wasn't happy with that explanation, and he reached into the box to pick up the doll. As he did, it squelched. I had no comparison as a child, but it was the sound that raw chicken fillets make if you squeeze them together. Disgusted, Jacob flinched, and dropped the doll onto the floor.

It twisted in the air.

And landed on its feet with a squishy noise.

I don't know how long we stared at that doll for. Neither of us dared move. When Jacob finally moved to pick up the doll, the doll took a step forward too. This made Jacob flinch back, yank his hands away, and the doll copied him on the floor, stumbling back then raising its little stumps defensively.

"Pick it up!" Jacob screamed.

I tried to calm him down - we were supposed to be keeping quiet - but my brother was being hysterical.

"Pick it up!" he screamed again, his voice high-pitched and terrifying.

I did it. I reached down and picked up the little doll. It was moist and soft in my hands. It made that same sickening squelch as I placed it down in its box. Jacob paced around the room, head in his hands, babbling to himself so fast and so quietly I couldn't hear what he was saying. I couldn't take my eyes off the walnut box. It wobbled around as the doll walked into its edges, trying to imitate Jacob's movements in what tiny space it had. I didn't really understand why Jacob was so scared. I was glad the doll was back to normal and alive again. We might have lost Mama, but at least we had the doll.

"Did Mama fix you?" I asked him.

The doll stopped pacing, looked up at me and nodded.

To my side, Jacob let out a sheer animal yelp of fear. He toppled onto the floor, kicking himself away to curl up against a wall.

"It made me move!" he cried, lips quivering, tears streaming down his face, "it made me move!"

I looked inside the box. The doll was imitating Jacob perfectly, pushing backwards and shaking with fear. I didn't truly understand, I was just a little girl, but my brother's fear was enough to make me close the box and encase the doll in darkness. Without knowing what to say, I did the only thing I knew how and curled up next to my brother, hugging his arm as he cried like a baby. He was always the strong one. Always the protector, who knew what to do next. God knows I didn't. We must have sat together like that for a long time. Eventually, he composed himself and said "we need to hide it somewhere."

He stood up, sliding free from my grip and nodded to himself.

"We need to hide it somewhere nobody will ever find it."

And he did. Jacob made me stay upstairs in the flat whilst he went out. He refused to tell me where he'd go, but he was gone for three hours. When he came back, it had just started raining, and his clothes were wet. He didn't say anything as I helped him undress. But when he lay on the mattress, I wrapped the duvet around him, as he had done so many times for me. He met my eyes then, and smiled.

"Love you," he whispered.

We fell asleep hugging, and when I woke up, for the first time in my life, I was alone.

No mother. No Jacob. The front door was still ajar. Our singular room had felt small all my life, but in that moment it felt impossibly large and daunting. I searched the flat for him, I walked the halls, I cried. Mrs Cooper eventually rang the police and I stayed at hers until they arrived. Of course, it didn't take long for a picture to be painted. Missing boy. Abandoned girl. I never saw my mother again.

Turned out I had an Auntie though. I stopped with them that night, and I never said a word. Especially not when I found out Jacob was dead. Years later, I would learn police found him floating face down in the canal. It got recorded as an accidental death; just another kid who ran away from home, slipped into the waters and couldn't climb back out. But I knew the truth. Jacob wouldn't run away, not without me. It had been the doll. Jacob threw him away, so he had thrown Jacob away. Mama Jane had pulled out his insides, so the doll had done the same to her.

My Auntie had a huge flat, and I got to sleep in the bed whilst she stayed on the sofa. I'd never slept in an actual bed before, but that night I didn't really appreciate the experience. My body clearly did though, as I fell asleep not long after my Auntie wished me a good night and turned the light off.

I dreamed that night. A vivid dream that I was walking down a cold, wet street. The glare from the lamp posts above me made me want to blink and squint, but for some reason I couldn't, and they were impossibly large, towering over me. One hand was behind me, dragging something. For a long time, I just kept walking, but some numb part of my mind wondered what I was dragging. I turned, and met Jacob, staring at me with wide, glassy eyes. He was sat upright, and I was dragging his coffin. It was filled with dark, dirty water up to his shoulders.

The sight of it was enough to shock me out of my dream. I wanted to sit upright, throw my covers off and find my newly discovered Auntie. But I couldn't move. I couldn't even blink. Locked in position, all I could do was stare at the ceiling and wonder why it felt like there was ground beneath my feet, even though I was lying down in bed.

Then my arm moved. It's a difficult sensation to describe. It was like cramp, or a spasm, without the pain. My muscles were moving, but I wasn't in control. I couldn't even try to wrestle with it. I couldn't strain or fight it. I could only watch as my right arm lifted, bending at the elbow. My hand formed a fist, and as though I were knocking on a door, my hand 'knocked' the air.

There was the faintest little 'tap tap', perfectly in time with my gesture. Then my paralysis melted away and I was back in control. After flexing my fingers and wiggling my toes, I threw back the covers and looked around the room. Something had made a noise, and I couldn't figure out what it was. I looked under the bed and inside the drawers, opened the cupboard and climbed the table to search the shelves. As I walked back to the bed, something took hold of me and my entire body went rigid. Again, my hand made a fist and raised to knock on nothing at all. I let out a little whimper, not wanting to scream and wake up my auntie. As my knuckles rapped on the air, once again I heard the faint 'tap tap'. This time I realised where it was coming from.

The window.

I was released again, and almost fell to the floor as my

muscles struggled to adjust to my sudden regained control. The curtains were drawn over the window, and I made my way over, slowly peeling them back. It was so dark outside it was hard to make anything out, but the dim orange haze from the street lights at least let me see there was something on the exterior window sill.

A walnut box. Open. And staring through the window at me were two glinting black button eyes.

My brother's killer. Mama Jane's killer.

The doll had come back for me.

How had it got here? Had it been controlling me while I slept? Walking down the dark streets of Liverpool, dragging its wretched box and making me dream of coffins?

We watched each other for a long time. It didn't take control of me. That made me think it was waiting to see what I did. Jacob and Mama Jane had been retaliation for the way they treated it.

As quietly as I could, I opened the window, and carefully pulled the box through, doll still standing inside. My hands were shaking so much that it would have made a normal doll topple over. But even though the walnut box trembled in my hands, the doll stood completely still.

I closed the window. The doll was drenched from rainwater, and with the window shut I could almost feel the stench rising upward. I lowered until our eyes were inches apart, then kissed him softly on the top of his hessian head. It was wet on my lips, and the smell was unbearable. As I stared into his empty black eyes, one of my earlier names for this doll slithered into my thoughts.

"Goodnight, Mr Buttons," I whispered.

Picking the doll up, I laid him tenderly down in his box -

trying my best to ignore the squelch - and found a little dust cloth to wrap around him like a bedsheet. Closing the box, I hid it under a few papers in one of my Auntie's drawers. I went to bed, but didn't sleep.

By the end of the next day, when nothing bad had happened, I repeated my actions of the previous night. Open the box, take out Mr Buttons, wish him "good night", tuck him in, close the box. The kissing was the hardest part, and the smell, but I'd hold my nose and keep a tissue to wipe my lips. When it kept working, I kept doing it. I've done it every night since Jacob's death. On Christmas eve. After nights out with friends. My wedding night. I still do it to this day. Jacob's birthday is always the hardest, but I don't even need to force myself to do it anymore. In fact I think it will feel strange to stop.

I never told anyone about any of this, because even as a child I knew nobody would believe me. But now my husband has found the box. We want children soon. What if they find it one day? It's too horrible to even think about. I've been trying to decide what to do all day, but my mind is finally made up. Jacob and Mama hurt the doll, but they didn't destroy it. It only took revenge after they'd done something to it. But if I destroy it, completely and utterly remove it from this world, it wouldn't be able to take its retribution against me.

That's my plan, anyway. If it doesn't know what I'm planning, it won't be able to get revenge. But I don't know how any of this works. I never have.

I have to try. For my husband. For my future children.

Tonight, I'm going to kiss the doll good night, as I always do. I'm going to tuck him in and close the box. I'm going to wait for my husband to fall asleep and creep downstairs. And then I'm going to burn that fucking box, with the doll inside.

I'll wait until it's nothing but ashes, and then I'll pour more petrol on the flames. I'll watch it burn all night. For Jacob. For Mama. I'm going to end this horrible doll once and for all.

Goodnight, Mr Buttons.

**Item 020**

**"OODOOV"**

[retrieved following house fire at [redacted], Liverpool]

# Item 020

Although Containment Cell 020 was no larger than those surrounding it, the miniature occupant within made it seem vast and imposing. A crude doll, made from a hessian sack. Its stumpy limbs were stitched onto its body and black button eyes reflected the harsh light inside its cell. It must have been less than a foot tall, but this didn't seem to affect its permanent black-thread smile. Pressed against a wall, it marched endlessly forwards, even though it had run out of space to move. Step, step, step, pushing its little body into the wall, seemingly oblivious to the barrier, as though it were trying to pass right through it. Step, step, step. Step, step, step.

It made no sound as it moved, save for the whisper-faint scratching of its buttons and limbs against the concrete wall. After a while though, approaching footsteps came from the corridor outside, stepping in time with the little doll. Two figures walked past the glass, and as they reached the door, the little doll turned its back on them, and lifted one of its hessian arms, as though pushing an invisible button. There was a soft beep as one of the figures outside pressed a finger onto the security scanner, and the containment cell unlocked with a hiss of hydraulics.

The door swung open, revealing a man and a woman in white lab coats. The man was collecting two pairs of blue rubber gauntlets which hung to the side, but as he passed a set to the woman, she shook her head.

"I'm a bit late for those now, look."

She pointed at the little doll, and it raised a stumpy arm ahead of itself in imitation of her. The man froze with rubber gloves outstretched, eyes darting from the doll to the woman, comparing them. With a bemused expression, he took hold of the woman's other arm and lifted it. The doll's arm did the same. He let go, and both arms dropped back down. Finally, he pursed his lips and placed one set of gloves back.

"Suit yourself," he said, donning his safety gloves, blue rubber covering his hands and forearms all the way to the elbow.

They walked into the room, and the doll walked away from them, matching the woman step for step. She was five or six times the size of the doll though, and her longer footsteps let her quickly catch up.

"Hello Oodoov," she said with forced cheeriness, as she gently picked the doll up. She moved into the centre of the cell, the doll's legs waggling in midair, still copying her footsteps. Its arms were bent, as though it clutched an even smaller version of itself in its own hands. She absent-mindedly stroked the dolls head, as the man fumbled with a clipboard in his gloved hands. He was trying to turn the first page - a series of safety warnings typed in bold and underlined - but the fingers of his gloves were too thick to separate the pages.

"Swap?" the woman suggested after a moment.

"Please," said the man, offering the clipboard with a sheepish grin.

There was a sharp contrast as they exchanged the doll. The woman might have been holding a newborn baby. The man looked like he had just been passed an anthrax bomb. He took hold of it gingerly, and held it at arm's length, frowning at it.

"What have they got us doing to you today, hmm?" he cooed.

"Something horrible, I imagine," muttered the woman,

flicking through the pages of the clipboard. "Josh had to set fire to the poor thing last week."

"Bloody hell..." said the man, shooting her an uneasy look. "How's Josh now?"

"Restrained. But recovering. I've told him he should put in a grievance complaint, but I think he's afraid that will just upset *Lord* Auburn."

The man chuckled, and glanced over his shoulder to make sure they were alone. "He's not wrong. Upsetting Auburn is exactly what landed me Oodoov testing in the first place."

"How did you upset him this time?"

"Same as every time. Disagreed with him."

"You too, huh?" The woman found the page she was looking for and read it aloud. "Experiment X54-020-008. Research staff are to repeatedly expose Item 020 to a non-harmful situation that would be stressful to a human being, but should have no impact on the Item itself. Using the provided container..." She trailed off as she read ahead. "Oh god. They've got us waterboarding it."

The man tilted his head from side to side, weighing up this information. "Well, it doesn't need to breathe, does it? Maybe it won't mind getting a bit wet."

The woman held a palm out in front of the doll's threaded smile, took a deep breath then blew out a heavy lungful. Apparently not feeling any air come from the doll's mouth, she shrugged.

"Maybe," she said, though she didn't sound convinced. "I'll go grab everything."

As she left the containment cell, the man glanced at the doll in his outstretched hands and gave it an awkward smile. "Sorry about this."

He tried his best to quietly explain the situation to the doll. That it wasn't their idea. That they were being forced to do this, and they didn't want to and they were really sorry. He meant it too. The doll smiled back at him with unblinking black button eyes.

It didn't take long for the woman to return with a small trolley carrying a large transparent tank, filled almost to the brim with cold water.

"I just don't see what Auburn wants to prove here," said the woman as she pulled the trolley to the centre of the cell. The water sloshed against the sides, droplets spraying to the floor. "We already know it retaliates if something is done to it."

"He wants to find the limit," said the man, resignation heavy in his voice. He stepped forwards and held the little doll above the water tank. Its rippling surface shimmered in the glare of the lights above. "Fire hurts it, so it hurts back. But water shouldn't harm it. What do you think will happen?"

The woman looked from the doll to the water, then sighed. "I don't know," she admitted.

The man shrugged. "Then we test."

The woman paused, eyes on the little doll. "Can you... Would you mind if... Could you...?" She trailed off.

"Do the dunking?" suggested the man.

"If that's ok. It's just its linked to me, and-"

"It's fine."

Nodding gratefully, the woman walked to an intercom panel near the door. Pressing her index finger to a small scanner, she spoke aloud. "Researcher Katie Harper. Containment Cell 020. Experiment in progress."

Above the door, a yellow light immediately illuminated, bathing the cell and the corridor outside in a warm summer tinge. The door hissed as it closed shut, sealing both researchers inside. Two discreet surveillance cameras now displayed a static red dot, and Katie straightened under their unblinking stare. She spoke aloud again, addressing the air, knowing her every word was being recorded.

"Experiment reference X54-020-008. In attendance are researchers Katie Harper and Dylan Jones. Notes and hypotheses can be found in the corresponding report. We will now submerge Item 020 in water, for as long as a linked individual can hold their breath. Experiment will be repeated indefinitely."

"Submerging," said Dylan, his words squeezing past gritted teeth. He forced the doll head-first beneath the surface, until even its legs were beneath the water. As he did so, Katie took a big gulp of air, and held her nose with her free hand.

The doll didn't kick or struggle. Its black thread smile didn't slip. It remained perfectly still, one stumpy arm pressed where its nose would be, still copying Katie.

Rubber gloves held out as far as he could, Dylan glanced from the doll, to Katie, watching for any signs that something might be wrong. Nothing changed.

Eventually Katie nodded and let out a breath, as Dylan pulled the doll from the water. It was drenched, water soaking in through its hessian skin, dripping onto the floor. As they both stared at the doll and waited, a lingering, uncomfortable pause settled over them.

"Again?" asked Dylan, and at a nod from Katie, he plunged the doll beneath the surface again. "Submerging."

Katie held her breath. Dylan watched through gritted teeth. The doll smiled.

A gulp of air announced the limits of Katie's lungs and the

doll was pulled out. Dylan examined it as streams of water dribbled from its stumpy legs.

"No reaction. Again?"

"Again."

Gulp. Dunk. Hold. Breathe.

They repeated the process. Over and over. Until the doll was a sodden rag.

"No reaction," said Dylan. He almost sounded disappointed.

"I think we can conclude, don't you?"

"..." Dylan paused a little too long.

"You want to keep going?" asked Katie, a note of indignation in her voice.

"Well, it's... I think you could hold your breath longer."

"I'm holding it as long as I can..."

Dylan opened his mouth to argue, then snapped it shut. He seemed to wrestle with himself a moment, then took a deep lungful of air. For a long minute, the two researchers stared at each other in silence. The only sound in the room was the drip-drip of water falling from the doll to the concrete floor of its cell. Then Dylan raised one rubber gloved hand into the air. He nodded to himself. He frowned. His face began to grow red. His cheeks bulged. After a long moment, he broke and took in a sharp, heaving gulp of air.

Once he'd caught his breath, he said "I raised my hand when I wanted to quit, but I didn't stop until I needed to quit. See the difference? You're stopping at the first one."

Their faces momentarily traded colour as Dylan's skin returned to normal and Katie's flushed a hot pink. Sparing a brief glance for the surveillance cameras, Katie swallowed down whatever words she held on her tongue, and simply said "OK."

Avoiding Katie's gaze, Dylan held the little doll above the water, both hands outstretched. "When you're ready."

A deep intake of breath acted as a starting gun, and the doll was plunged once more beneath the water. Dylan held it there, grim determination on his face, shooting cautious glances at Katie as she held her breath, cheeks puffed out.

Time silently ticked away, marked only by the gently sloshing water that lapped lazily at the sides of the tank. Even Dylan's breathing was quiet, as though he were trying his best not to rub it in. Soon enough though, Katie reached the point where she had broken before, and she kept going. Now and again, her lips would tighten, and fresh breaking points painted themselves across her face. But she kept going. She shut her eyes as her face began to darken. But she kept going. For a moment, it felt to her as though she were inside that glass tank, pinned beneath the water. But she kept going.

Then her leg twitched, kicking out in a spasm. Her eyes went wide. Dylan's did too. Had it been Katie who had moved? Or the doll? Keeping his eyes focused on the little figure in his hands, Dylan barely noticed Katie step forward. Perhaps he thought the doll was thrashing. When Katie put her hands on his arms though, he looked up. Rasping noises barely escaped her throat, nostrils flaring out desperately. She forced his arms out of the water, snatching hold of the doll, and before Dylan could react, she had pulled it from his fingers and pushed it into his face. He flinched as cold, wet hessian rubbed against his skin, first recoiling from the disgusting physical sensation, then lurching back as he realised the larger implication. Now, he was linked too.

"WHAT ARE YOU DOING?" he shrieked, stepping away so fast he almost fell backwards. "What the hell are you doing?!"

As he threw his arms around in exasperation, the doll in

Katie's arms copied him, gesticulating wildly.

Katie was purple in the face now, and her head tilted back as she sucked in desperate lungfuls of air. Shaky, trembling breaths that shook her whole body. "It... it wasn't me," she spluttered between convulsive bouts of panting.

Dylan threw off his gloves and shouted out loud, keeping to the edges of the cell as he attempted to storm out. "For the record, researcher Katie Harper has just exposed me to Item 020."

"It wasn't me," Katie managed weakly, still heaving as she tried to catch her breath. The doll in her hands moved its stumpy legs, walking quickly in mid-air.

The cell door opened with a wretched hiss. Dylan marched out of Cell 020 and out of sight.

"It wasn't me..." Katie whispered, still clutching the doll. Water dripped to the floor, and its black button eyes glinted in the light. For a while, Katie just stood there. Then, she set the doll down on its feet, apologised, and walked towards the open door. The doll followed her, still coping Dylan's unseen strides, but its steps were too small to make the distance.

"Experiment end," Katie said aloud, as she turned back and locked the cell doors with a quick swipe and a few buttons. She turned away as the doll hit the glass and kept walking forwards, wet hessian stumps pressing into the glass, smile on display for anyone in the corridor to see.

But there was nobody.

Katie's footsteps soon faded away, and the doll was alone once more. Water still oozed out of its stumpy feet, and its occasional movement shook dirty droplets free. After a while, the doll seemed to slam an invisible door, and sit down in empty space, stumpy hands clutching its head. Still copying

Dylan's every move.

But then something changed. It stood, and walked further into its cell. It opened another invisible door, then leaned forward. Its stumpy arms moved in precise, angular motions. Hard to say exactly what its counterpart might be doing. Putting a plug into a bath, perhaps? Turning both taps to full, maybe?

Then it waited, looking slightly down. As though it were watching an invisible bath fill up. All the way. To the brim.

It waited.

And waited.

And waited.

Then it plunged its head in, and held it down.

Of course, in the little doll's cell. There was no bath. The only water was still inside the glass tank, which was untouched. But it held its head in place. Not moving a muscle. The doll didn't have any, after all.

It held it for some time. About as long as a person might need to breathe. Not want. Need.

Then it removed its head. Waited. Then lowered it again.

And again.

And again.

And again.

Then, as though a spell had ended, it fell backwards, pushing itself away with stumpy legs, its hessian shoulders shaking, stumpy arms clutching its face, as though it were uncontrollably sobbing.

Throughout the whole experiment, and this subsequent revenge, nobody had paid any attention to a man in a chequered-suit, sat on a plump red leather chair, silently reading his book. Perhaps he had been reading so quietly, nobody had noticed him. But now, he peeled his eyes away from the page and looked down at the little doll.

"Spiteful little thing, aren't you?" The Narrator said.

The doll turned, and looked up at him with black button eyes and a stitched on smile. After a moment, it shrugged.

The Narrator picked it up, delicately between finger and thumb, and placed it on his thigh. The doll sat like a child on Santa's lap.

"I suppose we all want vengeance sometimes. The smallest of us, most of all..."

The doll nodded.

"Still..." The Narrator said, returning his book and grabbing the one next to it, "this has reminded me of a story. Would you like to read it?"

The doll looked up at The Narrator, then to the book. It nodded, and reached for the book with stumpy hands.

"No grabbing..." The Narrator held it out of reach. "You'll soak the pages."

# “Confessions of a London Flusher”

*[ posted on internet forum by potential witness ]*

You kids like scary stories eh? I’ve read the waffle you lot call stories - made up creatures and boogeymen. Never had anything to be afraid of, that’s your problem.

Why don’t you get comfy and let this old timer tell you a proper ghost story.

I was born - and I will die - in the City of London. The British Empire was the heart of the world for a reason, and believe you me - that heart is still ticking over just fine. Even if it does cost a ruddy fortune to live here these days. I’m lucky. Got in early, didn’t I? Couldn’t buy a shed in someone’s garden if I had to start over.

Tried a few different jobs when I was a lad - just how it was back then - but the one that stuck was a flusher. Working underneath the hustle and bustle, deep in the belly of London. In the sewers. You know how sometimes you get a clog in your toilet and you have to get a plunger or even a coat hanger to get rid? Imagine that for a whole city. Well, I was London’s coat hanger.

“Sewage technician” they call us now. Daft if you ask me. Nothing technical about it. But I was a flusher (or a “sewage technician” if you want to get all airy fairy) for over thirty years. So I’m sure you can believe me when I say I’ve seen some shit. It's mad what people flush away, and in the damp darkness, everything looks different. Between me and the lads, we had a lot of stories.

One in particular stays with me though.

I was that ripe old age where you start realising you're past your best. Before your knees creak and your back gives out, and you start finding out what old really is. I'd been around a while. I'd seen it all. Or at least, I thought I had.

Started out just like any other day. Blockage in the system, City Council couldn't fix it from up top, so they sent us down. Me and Charlie pop out in the van, lift the manhole, slap some traffic cones around it. We have a quick game of rock, paper, scissors, and I lose. That means Charlie's topman, and I have to strap my gas detector on and head down.

Stepping down the ladder rungs, daylight disappears.

If you've never been underground then you're not missing much. It's hot, it's dark, and it bloody stinks. After a while though, you get used to it. Give it long enough, and the stink starts making you hungry.

"I could murder a kebab," I radioed in to Charlie when my feet touched the bottom of the catch pit. Water was flowing fine through this section. It was a relatively modern part of the network, everything was made of concrete; cheap and quick. I already knew which way to head - the blockage was further upstream. Keeping my headlight trained on my feet, I started making my way towards the blockage.

"Just a sandwich for me today mate," came Charlie's voice through my radio. "I'm trying to look after my heart, not stuff it full of donner meat."

"Yeah, yeah," I said, knowing full well how much he'd moan when I had a tray of the stuff stinking up the van later.

He'd been sticking to his guns since his New Year's resolution, and I'd always suspected his wife was behind his sudden obsession with diet. Eating had always been the highlight of our day, before she'd twisted his ear. Still, it wasn't going to stop me from stuffing my face with a tray of greasy meat, chips and garlic mayo.

Ducking my head to squeeze through a tight culvert, I had to scrape my hi-vis jacket against the pipe wall to avoid stepping in the steady stream of water. Dark shapes bobbed up and down, piercing the surface as they flowed past - unwanted rubbish, dead leaves and rogue turds. I risked a glance ahead, and saw a pair of rats scampering away from my headlamp. Good thing about rats was they didn't want anything to do with you either. And some of the bastards grew big enough down here to fight alley cats and come out tops.

Eventually I made my way into an old brick chamber, a junction where the pipe split in two. One of the pipes still had that same stream of water flowing through, the other was bone dry. No prizes for guessing where the blockage was. What did puzzle me though was why this chamber wasn't on our plans. Normally any junction of pipe had an access chamber, but then by the look of the crumbling brick and dusty mortar, this had been here some time. As the trickle of water echoed off the walls, I glanced up, and my light disappeared up the beginning of an access. Squinting, I thought I could see more brickwork at the top. It was hard to tell from this far down, but I guessed it had been blocked up and forgotten some time ago. London is one of those cities that was built on top of itself, over and over. Old chambers like this were nothing I'd not seen before.

The dry pipe was even smaller than the one I'd just come through. Rather than just duck my head, I had to crouch and waddle through with my shoulders sideways. With just the soft beep of my gas detector to keep me company, I found myself hoping the blockage wasn't building up. Normally there would be at least a dribble coming down the pipe. If something had completely plugged the pipe, the job would become vastly more dangerous. Getting shit on your boots was one thing, drowning in sewage was something else entirely.

My fears were put to rest when I heard the faint sounds of trickling water ahead. Turned out there was no blockage at all. A brick weir had collapsed, and took a section of pipe wall with it. Water flowed through the collapsed brickwork into darkness below, which had now become the lowest point in the pipe run. Instead of flowing normally, water caught the rubble of the weir, so everything was diverted away.

As I took a closer look, I wondered how long it had been like this. It must have been some void to take the constant flow of water and not fill up. I clambered over the pile of decaying bricks, thankful that at least it was an easy fix. I'd been expecting a fatberg - an unholy build up of congealed fat, rubbish and human excrement. I'd take bricks and rubble over that abomination any day of the week.

"Looks like there's been a collapse," I radioed in to Charlie, taking my gas detector off and placing it near the opening where water was still gushing through like a waterfall. That was the next risk, that wherever the water was going might have unearthed some deadly release of methane or CO2. Even too much oxygen could cause problems. My little gas monitor could pick up any of the big four that could kill me, so I left it to check the air as I waited back in the pipe. I'd seen rats come that way, so knew it was safe enough. Another reason I didn't mind seeing rats down here. If they were alive, I should be fine too. At least for a while.

"Big job?" asked Charlie's crackling voice through my radio.

"I can clear it," I replied. "Just doing a gas check first."

After ten minutes of idle chit chat over the radio, the gas detector hadn't picked up anything, so I started clearing some of the debris, tossing bricks up to the walkway with a clatter. Before long, most of the water was heading back down the pipe, and I used the rest of the bricks to form a make-shift dam around the collapsed hole. With the problem fixed, I let curiosity get the better of me and had a peek down the hole. My headlamp revealed more brickwork - a whole separate section of Victorian sewers that looked long abandoned. Back in the day, they didn't just use these tunnels for waste. Canal boats would pass through, transporting coal, clay, silk and everything else an 18th century Englishman could flog. I have to admit a bit of a personal interest in this sort of thing, and with the hole big enough and easy enough for me to climb down, it was far too tempting not to clamber down for a proper look.

There was a whole world down there, a golden age of forgotten infrastructure. And once we'd phoned in the problem, we'd never get to see this again, it would just be bricked up by a construction team and abandoned once more. Since I knew there were no gases to worry about, I couldn't miss the opportunity to see it for myself. Snatching up my gas monitor, I let Charlie know what I was doing. "Just having a cheeky butchers, Charlie."

"Be careful mate," warned Charlie, but I was already halfway down. Shards of bricks clattered and tumbled under my unsteady feet, dust swirling in the air wherever my headlamp pointed. Once it drifted to the edges of my light, it was like it stopped existing.

Down in the canals, the air was dank and stale. But there

was a feeling there too, something I could barely sense. Sewers were mundane to me, every day. This was exciting, but more than that was a sensation that I was intruding. Unwelcome. It was enough to make me want to scramble back up to normality. But as I twisted my head left and right, I saw something.

The faint glow of my headlamp glinted off something in the tunnel ahead. Something in the canal itself. Leaning over the edge, I could see that most of the water had drained away, and what would have once held metre deep water now just had a steady trickle of waste water.

No rats down here, just my gas monitor, softly beeping every few seconds to remind me it was working. I stuck to the walkway, and moved towards the shape in the distance, still catching the reflection of my headlamp. As I got closer, I could make out a fairly large and blocky shape. My footsteps echoed, bouncing off the walls and making every sound louder. The gurgling sewage, the faint drips of leaking water, even my own breathing.

Finally, I got close enough to see it. A bathtub, filled to the brim. It must have been tossed in the canal, hundreds of years ago, but it still looked in decent nick. I unclipped my gas detector and gave it a cautious wave inside the canal. Nothing.

I clambered down to get a proper look. "There's a bathtub down here Charlie," I said over the radio.

Without missing a beat, Charlie's voice shot back. "Oh good, you can have a wash for once."

Clambering down into the canal, I turned my head to shine the headlamp over it. The bath was freestanding, with pristine silver feet. Despite their age, they still shimmered in the dim light. Other than being full with century-old canal water, it looked fashionable enough to make my own tub back home look like a bucket of crap. True to my cockney roots, I let out an impressed whistle as I got close enough to touch.

The water inside - if you could call it water - was jet black. It made the sewage trickling beneath the tub look clean enough to drink, and seemed to devour the light of my headlamp. What puzzled me most was it seemed to be spilling over the edges, dripping down. As if it was being filled from the inside. As I gazed into that pitch, rippling surface, spiderleg shivers ran across my back, and I felt cold even in my jacket.

Splashing footsteps made me flinch, and I twisted just in time to see a small shape running away from me before it disappeared into the darkness. Without realising it, I'd pressed my back into the canal wall, instinctively trying to escape. Yeah, I'll admit it, I was scared. But even though I'd only caught a glimpse, I knew what I'd seen. A child.

"Hello?" I shouted down the tunnel. My own voice came back at me, over and over, echoing down the tunnel. Staring into the fading light and squinting, I tried to convince myself I'd just imagined it. But I knew I hadn't. Part of me wanting to leave, part of me wanting to investigate, I found myself frozen, unsure what to do. If it had been a child, some poor sod who had fallen down here and got lost, I couldn't call myself a man if I left them down here to rot.

I bit my tongue and started down the canal in the direction whoever it was had disappeared.

"Hello?" I called again. Keen to hear anything except running water and my beeping gas monitor, I radioed into Charlie. "I think someone's down here mate."

"Don't play games with me Dan," he said back.

"I'm serious," I said, quickening my pace. I could hear splashing up ahead.

At the edge of my light, I saw it again, a small figure, running through the sewage.

"Hello?" I shouted.

The figure stopped running, and turned around. Barely visible, I could just make out the silhouette of a little girl.

"It's okay," I said, trying to keep the terror out of my own voice, as I raised my hands and took careful steps towards her. She said something, but she was too far away and it was lost in the tunnels. Charlie's voice crackled over the radio. "What's going on?"

I could see her properly now. A girl no older than eight, with long black hair and wearing a dingy, grey dress. She was barefoot. My hands were shaking as I dropped to one knee in front of her, and told her everything was going to be okay.

"Have you seen my mummy?" she asked, no fear or emotion in her little voice. She was dripping wet, her hair and her dress soaked to the skin. She must have been freezing, and I guessed she was in some state of shock. I can't remember exactly what I mumbled to her, something reassuring hopefully. I remember fighting the urge to ask her what the hell she was doing down here. The only important thing was getting her out.

"There's a fu- there's a little girl down here, Charlie," I stammered into my radio, as I slid off my harness and took off my jacket. I draped it around the little girl, hoping it might give her some comfort and warm her up a bit.

"I can't find my mummy," she said, in that same hopelessly tiny voice.

"Let's find her then, eh?" I said, trying to smile as I held out a hand. No doubt she couldn't even see my face. The only light in that entire tunnel was coming from the top of my head, probably blinding her. Even if she could make out something beyond a silhouette and a light, she probably could barely see me through that thick black hair, matted and stuck to her face with damp. Still, she took my hand. With fingers cold as ice, and as wet as if she'd just dipped them in a river.

I did my best to lead her and shine my headlamp on the moss covered brick floor ahead of her, and tried to make her feel safe - asked her what her name was, told her things were going to be okay now, but all she said were the same things, over and over. "Have you seen my mummy?" "I can't find my mummy."

I put it down to shock, until we came to the bathtub. As soon as my headlamp fell on it she tried to pull out of my grip. Not away from it, but towards it.

"Mummy!" she said happily, and grabbed hold of the rim, cocking one leg up as if she was about to climb inside. I managed to get my other hand around her waist and pull her back.

"Not in there darling," I said frantically as she squirmed and wriggled in my hands, trying to wrench herself free, "your mummy's not in there."

"Mummy!" she insisted, grabbing my forearm with icy hands and trying to pull loose.

Grabbing her with both hands, I lifted her up and walked away from the bathtub. She began to cry and beat her little fists at me, wailing for her mother.

"It's okay," I stammered, crying myself as I pulled her away, "it's going to be okay."

Once we'd got out of sight of the tub, she seemed to calm down. She hugged me and asked if I'd seen her mummy. "I'm taking you to find her, I promise," I said desperately, placing a hand on the back of her head and pulling her into my shoulder. Her hair was so wet, it felt like the water was coming out of her, dribbling onto me. I ignored it, and as we got to the break in the wall where I'd entered, I lifted her up onto the edge. She seemed to have forgotten all about the bathtub now, and calmly watched me as I hoisted myself up onto the walkway.

"I can't find my mummy," she said as I got to my feet and took her hand again. Even after walking, even with my jacket around her, her skin was still freezing. I worried that she might be too far gone, and quickened my pace, urging her up the toppled bricks into the sewer above.

"We're going to find her," I said through clenched teeth, "we're going to find her."

Helping her up the jumbled brickwork, I lead her down the tunnel. "We're coming up Charlie, we're coming back up."

I could tell by Charlie's voice he knew this wasn't a game or a joke any more. "Ok mate, I'm ready, I've got you."

Rats scampered away from us as I pushed the little girl ahead. All the while, she said the same things, over and over. "Where's my mummy?" "I can't find my mummy."

I was in tears long before we reached the catchpit with the ladder. True to his word, Charlie was ready. He'd set up the winch on top, and the cord was dangling down waiting for us. My harness was too big for the little girl, and the ladder rungs were too far apart for her to climb. I pulled the rescue cord down, wrapping it around the backs of her legs, trying my best to make a makeshift seat that wouldn't hurt her as it pulled her up. I'm not sure if it worked, but she didn't cry. Still, I decided it was best to support her as Charlie pulled her up.

"Jesus Christ," I heard his voice over the radio, and far above us, I could see his face in the distant manhole, looking down.

“She’s ready,” I said, “bring her up gently.”

“Where’s my mummy?” asked the girl, water still dripping down her face. I didn’t understand how that was possible. I must have been with her for twenty minutes, how was water still trickling down her hair? Dismissing it, I focused on lifting her up, taking the bulk of her weight so the cord didn’t dig in too tightly. As Charlie wound up the winch, I clambered onto the ladder rungs, propping the little girl on my shoulders as I climbed.

“Mummy...” she mumbled, head lolling.

Worrying she didn’t have long left, I pushed her up with all my strength, shouting “faster Charlie, faster!”

I looked up the ladder, to the opening above where daylight was just beginning to reach us.

And the little girl melted.

Turned to water before my eyes. Freezing water showered me, and the little girl was gone. I almost slipped from the ladder as I tried to grab her, but... there was nothing to grab. Even her dress vanished, turning to black slime as it fell down. All that was left was the cord. I stared up at it as it ascended away from me, Charlie still winding it up. My brain couldn’t process what I’d just witnessed, and I glanced down, around the tight walls around me, anywhere, trying to find her, but she was gone.

Charlie appeared in the hole of daylight above me, shouting “Where is she? Where’s she gone?”

I looked down at the concrete catchpit beneath me, trying to make sense of it. Did she fall? There was nothing down there.

“Get out Dan, fuck’s sake, get out!”

I don’t really remember the next part. I must have climbed

out, because I remember sitting on the street, Charlie frantically asking me what happened, where the girl had gone. I remember watching him climb down the manhole, and come back up empty handed.

"She just vanished," I mumbled when we were back in the van. I was still soaking wet, head to toe, drenched in the grimy water that the little girl had turned into. Charlie took me home, walked me indoors. Helped me take my clothes off and didn't even crack a joke. He made me a cup of tea and we just sat in my kitchen. Charlie would ask questions, but I didn't really know the answers.

We decided to report the collapse, but not the little girl. That would demand an investigation and we'd both sound mental at best, or child killers at worst. Just seeing things, we agreed. We'd both just been seeing things. Eventually, after insisting I was alright, Charlie left me to get some sleep. But I couldn't. I just lay there on my bed, in the dark, trying to make sense of it all.

Deprived of my sight, I could almost hear her. That small little voice. The trickling water. The gentle beep of my gas monitor. Those same words, over and over. "I can't find my mummy."

"I can't find my mummy."

"I can't find my mummy."

I sat bolt upright. It wasn't just in my head. I could hear her. Distant, faint, but it was real. Scrambling out of bed, I switched on my light, trying to find the little girl. I almost tore my room apart looking, until I realised where it was coming from.

The bathroom. From the plug in my sink, from the drain in my bath, bubbling up from the water in the toilet.

"Have you seen my mummy?"

"I can't find my mummy."

"Where's my mummy?"

I tipped up my laundry basket and shoved everything I could find into my sink and bath, shut the toilet lid, did anything I could to smother that little voice. It still came out, a faint muffled voice, calling for her mother. "I'm sorry," I cried, as I shut the bathroom door, and clamped my pillow over my head. "I'm sorry."

When I finally did go to sleep, I learnt a new phrase. Night terrors. Vivid dreams that feel real, that come with physical sensations. Apparently some people get them, but I never had. Not until that night. That night I dreamed I was drowning. Face down in a bathtub, a hand on the back of my head, impossibly strong, forcing me beneath the surface. I tried to grab at the sides, but my hands just slipped off. I thrashed as hard as I could, but I couldn't stop it. Somehow the bathtub was much larger, the hand on my head much bigger. As though I were a child. As though I was the size of an eight year old girl.

I can't say how long it lasted. It felt like forever. They say drowning is a peaceful way to go, but there was nothing peaceful about that dream. When I finally woke, back in my own bed, I was drenched in grimy, black filth. I wanted to wash, but - and this is hard to admit as a grown man - I was too scared to get into the bath. I wiped myself clean with a towel, using the kitchen sink and plenty of soap to wash the smell out of my hair.

I called in sick the next day. First time I'd ever done it, but the boss said it wasn't a problem. Said I could take as much time as I needed. It didn't help. I tried staying at a friend's house, but I still heard her little voice, coming out of the plug.

When I did manage to get to sleep, I had that same dream. It came on and off for weeks after. It wasn't any easier, but it never felt as long as the first time, and I was never covered in anything except my own sweat. Eventually, just like the little girl, it vanished as if it had never been there at all. Eventually, I felt brave enough to take my bundle of clothes out of the sink and bath. I even placed my ear to the plug, praying that I wouldn't hear her little voice calling out to me. I didn't tell anyone the full details, not even Charlie. I told him I'd dreamed I was drowning, but that was it.

What was really strange was... he said he'd had the same dream. Just once. Just the first night. And when I asked him if he was covered in anything after he didn't know what I meant.

It took months before I could go back to work, and even then I couldn't go down. Charlie was good about it. We didn't flip the coin any more. He went down every time from then on, God rest his soul.

A construction crew patched up the collapsed wall. We tried to seem casual when we asked if they'd seen anything weird, but they said they hadn't. And for a few years, that was it. It became our ghost story. Something we'd tell the new lads. That if they saw a little girl asking for her mummy they should run for the hills.

I wish I could leave it there. But one day, when Charlie came back up, he was white as a sheet and shaking. I had to pull him out of the hole because he couldn't climb out by himself.

"I saw her Dan," he whispered with wide-eyes. "I fucking saw her down there."

"What did you do?" I asked, my own hands trembling as I unclipped him and took him to the van.

"I ran like fuck."

We wrapped it up, and I drove him home, trying my best to return the favour, as he'd done for me all those years ago. Took him back to his wife, and wished him well.

That night I barely slept. Perhaps I was terrified I was going to have that dream again. Perhaps some part of me had hoped that after all this time, maybe it *was* just a story. Maybe we *had* just been seeing things. Dreamt it up.

Charlie wasn't at work the next day. That didn't surprise me. If he'd had the same dream as I had that first night, I knew I wouldn't see him for a week. But at lunchtime we got called back to the depot for some bad news.

Charlie had died.

Peacefully in his sleep, was what they told us, but it didn't take long for the rumours to start. Choked to death on his own vomit. Drowned in his own saliva. Murdered, some reckoned.

It was hard listening to people I used to call friends talking about it so openly. So trivially. Charlie was a good bloke. I hit my limit when I caught some of them asking "how can someone drown in their sleep?", and one of the arseholes had the nerve to laugh about it. Well, I launched myself over two tables to shut him up. Not often you see a man of sixty do something like that, I guess. Not often you see that same man punch out four teeth either. Nobody said anything about it after, not that I heard anyway. I wasn't around for much longer. "Early retirement," was what they called it.

At the funeral, Charlie's body went underground one final time. I gave my condolences to his family, even gave his wife a hug. Apparently there had been a police investigation into his death. When his wife had woken up, Charlie's body was covered in dirt, and the bed was wet through. Like he'd been killed outside in the rain, rolled around in mud, and brought indoors. But the police couldn't find any evidence.

'Inconclusive', they'd said.

I thought about telling her there and then. Telling her this story. But what good would it have done? It wouldn't have brought him back. It wouldn't have given her any comfort. So I kept quiet. Maybe that makes me a coward.

Maybe that's why I've felt like I've had to tell you lot. So at least someone knows. Even if none of you believe me.

We used to tell the new lads - if you ever see a little girl down in London sewers, run like fuck.

I'd tell them something different now.

If you ever see a little girl down in London sewers... Let her climb in the bloody bathtub.

**Item 303**

**“ABIGAIL”**

[recovered from London sewer system]

# Item 303

In the winding corridors of Floor Fifty-Four, two guards wrapped in body armour meandered towards each other. A coincidental mingling of their patrol routes. They both gave a subtle nod of acknowledgement as they got closer, and when the corridor branched off towards their shared break room, they fell into step besides each other.

Aside from their age, the most striking difference between the two guards was in the way they held themselves. The older of the two, Phil Jones, had an almost lazy saunter. His feet trod familiar ground, and his eyes gave one smooth sweep of the hall before falling on his comrade. The younger man was rigid, ready to fight his own shadow. He moved through the unknown halls with the look of a tourist bracing to get his wallet stolen. Maybe even his kidneys.

Phil surveyed the young man from the corner of his wrinkled eyes as they patrolled past the glass-fronted cells, weighing him up. Eventually he spoke, in a voice as casual as summer waves on a Cornwall beach.

"It's Tom, right?"

"Uhuh."

"How you finding it so far?" Phil asked.

Tom Nelly's gaze leapt from cell to cell, watchful and alert. One hand rested on his baton, and he looked poised to draw it out at the blink of an eye. "Weird," he eventually replied, "but I suppose it's sort of... easy? I mean, I've not really had to do anything."

"Same as everything," said Phil. "It's easy, until it's not.

Where'd you serve?"

"Hmm?"

"You've got soldiers' eyes, son. Where'd you serve?"

Tom finally peeled his gaze away from the cells. Briefly, he seemed to look inward. "Iraq. Basra, mainly."

Phil gave a small, humourless chuckle. "Small world."

"You too? Operation Telic?" the younger man asked skeptically. "Aren't you a bit old fo-"

"Gulf War, lad. Before you lot. Operation Granby."

"Aah," said Tom, with a growing smile, "we finished what you started."

"Finished, eh?" shrugged Phil. "If you say so. Personally I've never heard of any war ending without being a footnote in starting the next."

Tom nodded, smile slipping, eyes turning inwards again. For a moment, his fingers tensed, reaching for a rifle that wasn't there. He shook it off. "Keeps us in work, I guess."

For a while, the two walked in unison without saying a word. It was Phil who broke the silence.

"What landed you here then?"

Tom stumbled and came to an abrupt halt. He chewed on his words before he spoke. "What do you mean?"

Phil slowed his relaxed saunter, turned around and lowered his voice. "You know what I mean. You saw something. Or killed something. Something strange. Something you couldn't explain. And then they sent you here, and you find out that strange thing was just the pointy tip of the weirdo-iceberg."

For the first time, Tom's eyes slid away from potential threats in the corridor ahead and fell to his boots. "They told me not to talk about it."

"Yeah," agreed Phil, before pointing to the ceiling. "Up

there. On the surface. But we're both down here. We both know. Hell, we might have both seen the same bloody thing."

Tom's hand gripped his baton now, as if he planned on using it to knock the conversation aside. "They told me not to talk about it," he repeated through pursed lips.

Phil raised his hands and sidled around, continuing his patrol. "Suit yourself. Not gonna drag it out of you."

Tom fell back into step besides his older colleague, and as they made their way towards the break room, Phil flashed a grin that made him look twenty years younger.

"Wanna hear mine?"

Wrestling with his hypocrisy for a moment, Tom tilted his head back and forth before nodding sheepishly.

"Well, you served there, you'll already know it's hot as hell," Phil began, immediately launching into his story the moment Tom had shown willingness to listen. "Sun is bad enough, but you can feel the heat coming off the sand too. Cooking the air. Might as well be walking on a mirror. Only at least with a mirror you wouldn't end up with a beach-worth of sand in your boots every hour. Air so thick and hot, it feels like you're inside an oven, and God just keeps cranking up the dial."

"Yeah, and all that wrapped in body armour," agreed Tom.

"You lads were lucky, you had all that easy-breathe thermal shit. Top brass were convinced Saddam was going to gas us, so we spent half our tour stuck in chemical suits and gas masks. We were zipped up tight, and sweating so bad it would pool up to your bloody knees."

Tom winced. He didn't admit it, but his expression revealed he was glad he didn't have to wear those suits when he fought. He said nothing though, and let Phil continue.

"I don't know if it was a drill, or a balls-up, or what, but one day we were in the middle of a firefight and sarge yells at us to mask up. Apparently some twat had started shouting 'gas', but I never heard him."

They passed a cell containing a dusty floral sofa, with a scruffy man sat atop the cushions. This man thrust manacled hands up at them, following them as they walked, silently pleading for them to unclasp his chains. Both guards ignored him.

"As if it wasn't hard enough to see with the sun glinting off the sand," Phil continued, "now we had gas masks on, and every breath made the goggles steam up. All the while we're getting hotter, and hotter, and hotter."

The two guards came to a junction in the corridors, the cell nearest them housing a statue of an angel, frozen in the act of weeping. Real tears rolled down her marble cheeks. Ignoring her too, they turned the corner, walking around her glass enclosure. At the end of this alcove was a discrete door. Emblazoned in black text above the door frame were the words 'Outpost A'.

"There were six of us dug in, and we were still worried about sniper fire, so were keeping low," Phil said, placing his palm on the scanner at the door. "The first time I pop my head up, I see someone in the distance running towards us. Maybe half a click or less."

The door opened and Phil headed inside with Tom following behind. "So I call it out. Lay down some suppressive fire, but the guy doesn't stop. Even through my smeared up goggles, I can tell he's absolutely pegging it. Now he's getting closer, and I see he's unarmed. Not even wearing clothes. But he's covering some serious ground. Three hundred metres out. Two hundred. I'm trying to wipe my goggles, but I'm just making it worse.

I'm panting, pissed off, trying to see. One hundred metres out, the guy is still running full pelt. Then I notice he's got ginger hair. You don't meet many ginger Afghans, do you?"

As the two guards walked down a dimly lit, narrow passage, they stopped at another security door, with another scanner. This time though, Phil was too wrapped up in his story to swipe his handprint.

"I'm thinking, is he British? Yank maybe? Maybe he's running over here for help, right? But before I can say anything, Gaz unloads on the guy. Full clip. Right at him. Fifty metres away."

Phil licked his lips, eyes wide, revelling in his own memory. Reliving, as well as retelling. He shook himself, and placed his palm against the second scanner. "That's when we heard his footsteps. That's when we realised he wasn't fifty metres away at all."

The door opened, and Phil turned to go inside. "He was a..."

Abruptly stopping in place as the words died in his mouth, Phil only moved when Tom bumped into him from behind.

"What-" was all Tom managed to get out before he saw what had made Phil freeze.

Inside Outpost A, with its spread out chairs, grotty kitchen area and the faint musk of male body odour, was a little girl. Stood beneath a homemade banner that attempted to make the outpost feel more like a homely tavern than military quarters, the little girl shivered and stared up at the two burly guards with pitiful eyes. Her hair was so wet, it dripped onto the floor.

"H-have you seen my mummy?" she asked, lips quivering.

"Shit," muttered Phil under his breath. Suppressing a shiver, he moved towards the little girl and lowered himself into a crouch. "Hello Abigail."

The little girl gave a pitiful sniff, jet black hair plastered to her pale cheeks. Her cautious gaze crept above Phil's shoulders, and lingered on Tom. Baton clutched in both hands, Tom stared right back with eyes that didn't dare to blink.

Shooting a glance at his colleague, Phil gestured for the younger man to lower his weapon, and spoke once more to the little girl, as friendly and warm as he could muster. "Would you like me to take you back to your mummy?"

Only once Tom's baton was firmly holstered did the little girl return her attention to Phil. His words seemed to have done nothing to warm her.

"Do you remember me?" Phil tried, arming himself with a grandfatherly smile.

Wet droplets of black sludge flicked from Abigail's hair as she shook her head. Despite the mess splattering onto the floor, Phil sensed an opening and seized it. With an outstretched hand, and a grimace, he shuffled forwards onto one knee.

"I took you to your mother before, once. You can hold my hand, if you like?"

Wiping a tear from her cheek, Abigail gave the smallest of nods and grasped Phil's proffered hand. Her tiny grip could only fit around three of Phil's fingers. With a grunt, he pushed himself up, cursing his "goddamn knees".

As Phil turned to leave, his arm snagged back. The little girl wasn't moving. She was staring intently up at Tom, her face completely neutral. Her eyes seemed to drink him in; his armour, his weapon, his uncertain posture. It was an accusing stare that made the man feel like a boy. His head strained back and forth, trying to turn away, but his instincts wouldn't let him take his eyes off this little girl. This child that made his mind scream 'threat'.

A soft nudging from Phil's elbow shook him from his trance, and when Phil motioned to the girl with a tilt of his head, the cogs of Tom's mind finally began twisting into motion.

"Uhh..." Tom began, his throat feeling like someone was squeezing it, "Yeah. I'll... help."

After a consideration long enough to make Tom sweat, Abigail's gaze finally shifted away from him, and he could breathe again. The three of them walked out of Outpost A, back into the corridors of Floor Fifty-Four.

Phil's lazy saunter devolved into a patient escort as he matched pace with Abigail, leading but not dragging her.

"We're suppose to radio this in, right?" Tom asked, hovering on the peripheral and wanting to hurry this along.

"Yeah..." said Phil, keeping his eyes trained on the little girl. "But, I'm not sure if..."

A sharp metallic 'ting' resounded in the hallway as Tom unclipped his radio. The noise made Abigail halt and turn to stare at Tom again. She watched over her shoulder, no emotion showing on her face, but Tom felt those same sensations from before.

"...if that's a good idea..." finished Phil.

"Just checking it works," Tom told the little girl with a forced smile. The radio was promptly clipped back in place.

As they passed the corner cell, the angel statue wasn't crying anymore. Or at least, not that Tom could see. It was covering its face with both hands. He supposed it could have been weeping, but he felt more like it was afraid. Trying to hide the same way a child might. Abigail ran a damp finger across the glass as she passed, which squeaked and wailed, leaving a grubby trail.

The two guards escorted the little girl down the winding

corridors, and some of the inhabitants seemed to watch. Abigail watched right back. She wasn't crying now, or shivering. As they passed the sofa in Cell 042, an old woman sitting on the floral cushions waved and gestured to the empty seat next to her. Nobody waved back.

Turning around another corner, a young scientist walked towards the group. She looked up from her notes, and did a double take when she saw Abigail. If Tom wasn't covered in goosebumps himself, he might have smiled at the way she danced on the spot, cogs turning in her mind so clearly, you could almost hear them churning. Her instincts told her to run, but she knew the rules the same as everyone else. If you saw Abigail, you had to take her to her mother.

The scientist fell into step with the guards, clutched her reams of notes to her chest and hunched down to address the little girl. "Hello Abigail!" she said in a sing-song voice that did nothing to hide her panic.

"Have you seen my mummy?" replied Abigail, eyes watching her intently.

"I have!" squeaked the scientist, "she's not far away now!"

Abigail watched her a moment longer, then slowly turned back to the corridor ahead. The rest of the walk was silent, with the adults sharing brief glances of eye contact when they were certain the little girl wasn't looking. After a long walk that felt much longer, they came to a stop outside a glass fronted cell with a bathtub inside. Above the door, black letters glistened.

54-303

"Abigail"

Next to the door was an intercom. Tom moved to press it, but before he could reach, the scientist leant over and scanned her ID badge. With a hydraulic hiss, the door unlocked and swung ajar.

She scampered through, then Phil lead Abigail inside. Tom lingered at the door, gazing at the bathtub inside. It was freestanding, sculpted from pristine porcelain and mounted on elegant silver feet. No plumbing connected to the bath, and although there didn't appear to be any drains inside the Cell, the bathtub was full to the brim with black liquid. A droplet fell from one of its rusty, scum-stained taps and hit the surface, sending out ripples that danced and glistened in the sterile light above. Whatever substance was inside the bathtub, it moved somewhere between water and sludge, and the ripples quickly subsided, its surface falling deathly still. Under the harsh lighting, it almost looked like a slab of onyx, or a black mirror.

"Is that my mummy?"

The tiny voice made Tom jump. For a moment, his attention had been so absorbed into the darkness inside the bathtub, he'd forgotten there were other people in the room.

For a moment, none of them spoke. Tom looked at the other adults, hoping for clues as what to say, how to behave. The briefing had only said to bring Abigail to Cell 303, not what happened next. Perhaps Phil expected the scientist to take control, but judging by the way she examined the walls and ceiling - all the contents of the room except for the ones that mattered - that wasn't going to be happening soon.

With a cough, Phil leant over and said unconvincingly "yes, that's your mummy."

Abigail's lips weren't trembling now. Her little brow furrowed, still plastered with wet hair, still dripping onto the floor.

"Are you sure?" she asked in a voice so sweet, it made Tom want to cry.

Phil released a shaky breath, and stood up. "Yes, I'm sure."

The little girl looked at the bathtub, then turned to the scientist, who began frantically nodding. Little black eyes then turned to Tom, who gave a single bow of his head. It seemed to be enough.

Abigail let go of Phil's hand, and stepped towards the bathtub. As soon as he had it back, he began to rub the fingers she had been clamped on to all this time, trying to discretely blow on them and get some warmth back in.

"Her skin is like ice," he whispered as he joined Tom at the door.

A dainty hand ran around the rim of the bathtub, as Abigail circled it. Another drip from the rusty tap made the surface tremble. Abigail looked up and spoke once more. There was no accusation in her voice. No fear, or uncertainty. No emotion at all.

She simply asked, "Is this my mummy?", the same way she had spoken to them since she appeared.

"Yes," Tom heard himself say, the words escaping him like air venting from a pressure cooker. He nodded like his neck was on a well-oiled hinge, wishing and praying for this little girl to go away.

"Yes," the scientist said softly, "yes, that's your mummy."

"Yes, it is," agreed Phil.

With all three adults nodding at her, Abigail seemed satisfied. She climbed over the edge of the bathtub, dipping a tiny foot into the dirty liquid within. It disappeared, sending soft, black undulations across the surface. Abigail stood in the tub now, filthy black smears staining her thighs and the frills of her little white dress. Tom felt his hand rise towards her, felt an urge to wrench her out of that bathtub.

*Don't go in there Abigail,* Tom thought, *please get out, I'm sorry! This is wrong, you're just a child, you-*

"It's cold," said Abigail, as she began to sink. She watched the adults with glassy eyes as the black surface absorbed her legs, then her waist, before climbing up to her chest.

Tom clamped a hand over his mouth, but forced himself to watch. Phil watched right with him, his lips a tight line, all colour pressed out of them.

"I love my mummy," Abigail said, as the black water swallowed her shoulders, rose above her chin, smothered her lips. Her eyes met Tom's as they disappeared beneath the surface, and Abigail's head plunged completely into the dark liquid. A single black air bubble swelled to the surface, then popped, spraying droplets of filth onto the white rim of the bathtub.

The moment it was done, the scientist turned on her heels, muttering "I'm going to be so late." Her quick footsteps echoed down the corridor, but Tom couldn't take his eyes away from the black liquid that had smothered that little girl. A wrinkled hand pressed onto his shoulder, just light enough to feel through his armoured padding.

"Need a minute, huh?" Phil said, clearing his throat and nodding. For a moment both guards just stared at the bathtub.

Tom tried to say something, but no words came to him.

"Well, you've met Abigail now," said Phil. "It gets a little easier each time."

They left Cell 303, the door hissing shut behind them and locking tight. Tom shook himself and stretched his neck.

"Why did we do that?" he asked in a hushed whisper, blinking to keep his eyes from stinging. "Why did we let her go inside that... stuff?"

Phil resumed his casual saunter down the corridors of Floor Fifty-Four, back the way they'd walked. "Cos it's better than the alternative. Cos that's what we're supposed to do. Cos that's our job."

Tom gazed back through the glass into Cell 303. At the bathtub. At the water so black, not even the harsh lights could pierce through. "But where is she now? How often do we do this? Why-"

"Kid," interrupted Phil, with a deep sigh. "Leave the questions to the eggheads. We just keep everything inside its box. Less questions you ask, easier you'll find it."

A diode on their wrists began blinking at the same time, joined by a muted beep.

"Well, break time's over," muttered Phil with a bitter laugh, motioning for Tom to join him. "These halls aren't gonna patrol themselves."

With considerable effort, Tom peeled his eyes away from Cell 303, and fell into step besides Phil. For a while, they walked in silence. This time, it was Tom who broke it.

"I'd like to hear the rest of that story..."

Phil gave a wolfish grin, and as the two guards returned to their respective patrol routes, Phil rubbed at his chin and resumed his place. They passed a cell with a tiny hessian doll inside, sat on the lap of a man in a red leather chair. Together, both man and doll looked up from the book they were reading.

"I told you everyone loves a good story," the man said with a wink.

Snapping the book shut and placing it back on his shelf,

The Narrator plucked up the little doll and placed him back on the floor of Cell 020.

"Just the one for you though, I'm afraid."

The little doll folded its hessian arms and petulantly hunched its shoulders.

"Oh, don't sulk," said The Narrator, making a show of pouting his lower lip, and idly flicking it. "You know how upset they get if things go missing. Even for a moment."

He reached to his bookshelf, and plucked out a thick, leatherbound volume. "Things can only change in Floor Fifty-Four if they're supposed to change. If that's just the way they are..."

# “The Door with the Ivory Handle"

*[ extract from memoir, unpublished ]*

It’s strange how someone can have an impact on your life without being around.

For me, that person was my grandfather. I never knew him, never even laid eyes on him, and yet his absence in my family cast so large a shadow, it was almost a presence in itself. We would see him in my mother’s stiffened face, whenever we asked about him. We would hear him during my grandmother’s long silences; twisting her wedding ring in endless circles, staring into space. We would feel him in the walls of his great house, built from the fortunes of his antiques empire, his collection hidden away or shrouded from view. He did not feature in any of the empty photo frames, and yet even as a child, I knew it was his house. My grandmother just lived in it.

His employees still worked, hustling and bustling with deliveries. Items bought and sold in his name still brought money to my family. But there was a hole inside that house, and within our lives. A silence that screamed of betrayal, abandonment, and unanswered questions.

“Ran off with some young lass,” I overheard one of the movers say one day. He grunted as he lowered a chest of drawers, lacquered oak shimmering in the afternoon sun. My sister and I were playing hide and seek, so they had no idea I was eavesdropping. I stayed in my hiding place, peeking between ruffled dust sheets. There was a soft thunk as the legs settled on the polished wooden floor, and the men let out a sigh of relief. “That’s what I reckon anyroad.”

“Nah,” said the other voice dismissively, “you do that, you take yer money wi’ yer.”

My ears strained to wade through their accents. I knew exactly who they were talking about, and this sort of gossip was far more than I was ever likely to hear from any of my family.

“So what do you think then?” asked a more well spoken voice, the new boy, most likely. I had something of a crush on him.

“Summat dodgy,” said the dismissive voice. Another grunt, another thud. “Where you want this one?”

“Over by the grandfather clock please.” There was a pause and the new boy lowered his voice. “What do you mean, dodgy?”

“Come on lad,” heaved the dismissive mover through gritted teeth. They shuffled across the floor until I could barely see them, and plonked down the cabinet. “You don’t get this kinda cheddar wi’out doing someone rotten.”

“Ted thinks he were murdered,” said the first mover, resting a hairy arm on the cabinet as he caught his breath.

In my hiding place, I held my breath and shifted, trying to get a better view. Despite the July heat, their conversation made the air feel so very cold. I shivered and hugged myself.

“By who?” asked the new boy, then after a pause added “Take this one and... the cellarette over there.”

“Well, he were stealing from the Chinese, paying bribes to the Russians, undercutting the Americans and dodging taxes over ‘ere,” said Ted, as the men moved back into view. “And that’s just what we know about. Mark my words lad, we’ll open these crates one day and find what's left of him, stuffed inside. Just bones and teeth."

I closed my eyes and kept my tears silent. Abrupt laughter burst from the two gruff men, and at first I feared they could see me, but when I peeked back at them, they were watching the new boy, struggling with a cargo crate. They effortlessly plucked it from his arms and set it down on the trolley.

"Leave the lifting to us lad," Ted said as they carted the stock out the room. "You just tick them boxes."

Their chuckles faded away, and even when they were gone, I didn't cry out loud. Just clutched my knees and felt tears trickle down my cheeks. When Maisie found me several minutes later, I was still there, but I didn't feel like playing hide and seek any more.

"Why are you crying?" she asked quietly, tilting her head before shuffling over to sit next to me. She was three years younger than me, and was always such a tender soul. She leaned over and kissed my head softly, as though it would make me better. Like our mother would when we fell over and scraped our knees.

I didn't tell her, of course. I was far too protective for that. If I told her why I was crying, she would cry too. I wiped my tears away and flashed a smile. "Let's play something else."

There were plenty of games to play when we visited our grandmother. In a house that size, with countless treasures and mysteries, even an adult could lose hours exploring and perusing. Two little girls could play forever. We could dance in the empty rooms, or listen to our echoes in the cavernous hallways. We could live a million lives amongst the vintage furniture, trying on dusty top hats or having sword fights with silver-capped canes. We could drape ourselves in dust sheets, and pretend to be ghosts or birds or aeroplanes, running around with our flapping cloth cloaks trailing behind us.

But new stock bought new guessing games. Hidden under the sheets that covered them were antiques freshly bought, ready to sell or ready to be restored to former glories. It would be years before I learned the intricacies behind the business, but as a child, it was close to magic.

Most objects were easy; the sheets barely hid their outlines. But a blocky shape that looked like a table could end up being a stack of paintings, a freestanding chess board, or a sealed crate with yet more mysteries lurking inside. We made our way through the fresh inventory, but I let my sister pull off the sheets, and barely guessed myself, lost in thought. What if our grandfather *was* still inside one of these boxes? Desperate to get out. Trapped in the dark.

"Where are you going?" I heard Maisie ask.

My eyes focused, and I realised I was halfway out the door. Staring down the corridor, towards the door with the ivory handle.

Grandmother didn't have many rules for us to follow. Don't break anything. Don't irritate the staff. But the one she always insisted on was 'don't go into the room with the ivory handle'. She never explained why, she simply forbade it, quick and clean. I'd always figured there were valuables in there she didn't trust to children. The door wasn't locked, and I'd seen the staff go in there a few times, but only the most senior staff were allowed through this corridor.

Senior staff, and family.

I glanced back at Maisie and nodded for her to follow. She did so, and together we slowly made our way down the corridor, empty photo frames hanging ominously above us. I always wished they'd just put something in them. Photos of my mother, or us. Landscapes. Art. Anything really. Even taking them down would have been better than leaving them empty, like gilded tombstones.

Approaching the door, it was impossible not to feel small. The black panelled door towered over us, and had a way of looking heavy. Without having ever so much as touched it, somehow my mind knew the weight of it. With dry lips, I reached out to the handle. My fingers hovered, afraid it might burn to touch.

Footsteps made me snatch my hand away, and I turned on my heels, babbling nervous gibberish to my sister. Lucile, my least favourite administrator stalked past, her heels click-clacking. She ignored us completely as she passed. I don't think she cared for children, or not for us, at least. I always thought she looked shrivelled up, like a piece of fruit left out in the sun.

"Are we going to get in trouble?" whispered Maisie, after Lucile had left our view.

"No," I said with a smile, "of course not." But I knew it was too risky to try whilst the staff were still here. In a couple of hours, they would finish, and it would just be us and our grandmother. So I raced Maisie to the gardens and we practised cartwheels. But even in the summer sun, I couldn't get the image of my grandfather out of my mind, pressed in tight, clawing at the wooden insides of his box-shaped grave, pleading for us to find him.

The staff left at five o'clock, and we had dinner with our grandmother. Afterwards, we usually sat and did puzzles or drew pictures, but because the sun was still shining, our grandmother said we could keep playing outside if we wanted to. We did, but only until she took her eyes off us. Then we took off inside, sneaking towards the door with the ivory handle. The house was a different place with the staff gone.

Even in full daylight, it somehow felt larger and more foreboding. Maisie's fingers found my hand and held it as we walked.

The ivory handle glistened, as if inviting us. Looking closely, I saw it had golden leaves snaking around the outside and curling along its edges. Maisie squeezed my hand tight as I reached out and opened it, letting the door swing slowly open with a drawn out creak of rusty hinges.

There were no windows, and though I tried the light switch, the only light that trickled in was the creeping remnants of daylight, bouncing off the corridor behind us. It made the shadowy shapes within the room look dark indeed. Like a nightmare version of the guessing game we played. Maisie stood at the door as I crept inside.

She squeaked and I turned to see her pointing to my left. A hulking figure draped in a white sheet loomed over us. Peeking out from between the sheet were clumps of shaggy brown hair and giant, curled claws. Heart leaping, I braced for the monster to attack. Nothing happened. After a moment, I plucked up more courage than I knew I had, and slowly tugged at the dust sheet covering the monster. It fell away, revealing teeth and fur. My blood ran cold, if only for a moment.

It was a bear. Stuffed, and unmoving.

Behind me, Maisie giggled. She must have been emboldened by my display of temporary bravery, as she stepped to my side and joined me in unveiling the shapes within the dim room. Dust leapt into the air, swirling and making us splutter. One by one, the extravagant shapes were revealed. Patterned vases, golden toy soldiers, intricate galleons somehow placed within glass bottles. I could see why we weren't allowed in this room. Everything was fragile or delicate, and seemed like a toy to the eyes of young children. The thrill we got from unveiling each bizarre object even overpowered the melancholy mood that had hung over me like a black cloud, and I joined Maisie in smiling and giggling. We began to guess what the next shape was, before our eyes strained through to make it out amongst the fading light. One in particular caught my eye.

"It's a statue," I said. "A statue of a person!"

"It's not tall enough for a person," said Maisie.

"They're sitting down. Look," I pointed at what I thought was the head. "Nose, ears, mouth."

My finger traced the air, curving around the folds of fabric draped over whatever was hidden underneath. The way it hung made me convinced. A statue, or a shop mannequin. A large doll, maybe. The head and shoulders were a give away. Maisie was right though, it was too short, but the way the dust sheet also covered a blocky oblong beneath the person made me think of a park bench I'd once seen, with a statue occupying one seat and the other empty. I stretched out my hand, and just as my fingers settled on the fabric, whatever was underneath... shifted.

I flinched back, snatching my hand away and stumbling, my foot getting caught in the trailing sheet. I snagged it, and some of the dust sheet slid away, the rest getting tangled around the object underneath. Half revealed, barely lit by what little daylight trickled through the open doorway, was a sofa. My mind barely registered it, my eyes locked on what I thought had been a statue. Most of it was still wrapped in tangled sheets, but enough had been removed to show a trouser leg and polished black leather shoes.

Maisie stepped forwards to pull off the rest of the sheet, thinking it was another toy, like the bear, but I shot out a hand to stop her. It had moved. If it was a statue, it looked very, very real. And it had definitely moved.

"Don't-" I whispered to Maisie, but the moment the words left my mouth, they died. The folds of sheets twisted, the head of whatever was beneath snapping suddenly to face me. Maisie froze like a startled deer. We both watched the figure on the sofa, and it watched right back. Now I was looking closely, I could see it breathing, the sheets around its shoulders slowly rising and falling. Not daring to blink, not daring to speak, I gripped hold of Maisie's dress, forcing her backwards with me as I stepped slowly and carefully out of the room, never taking my eyes off the figure. It was so horribly, painfully clear to me now. It was a person. There was somebody hiding in my grandmother's house. Their head followed us, glacier-slow, and I desperately swallowed the instinct to sink down into a ball and cry. The dust sheet rippled and a section near the waist folded as whoever was underneath grabbed hold. They began to rise to their feet, dust sheet enveloping them like a spectre. I didn't stop to watch. With strength I didn't know I had, I physically lifted Maisie off the ground and ran, both of us screaming and crying so hard I could barely see where I was running. I didn't close the door or turn back to look. I didn't stop running until I found my grandmother. Didn't stop screaming and shouting until my mother, my father, and some of the staff showed up. Didn't stop crying until I fell asleep.

They never found anybody, of course. They searched the whole house. Nothing. No signs except disturbed dustsheets, all of which were blamed on me and my sister. Our parents had ended their night early to collect us, and whilst they were glad we were unharmed, we got the biggest telling off of our lives for going into the room with the ivory handle.

It was a long time until we were allowed to play unsupervised at my grandmother's house. When we went back, we were told the door with the ivory handle was going to be locked from now on. They said it as though they were trying to reassure us, but I heard the truth loud and clear - they didn't believe us. Maisie was happy though, she said she never wanted to go in that room ever again, and refused to even look at it, sometimes going around the house rather than walking past it. I wasn't satisfied though, and as the terror of the event slowly faded away, I began to consider another possibility. What if that person wasn't a stranger, hiding amongst the old relics? What if it was my grandfather, still alive, still visiting us and our grandmother? That would explain why the house always felt like his. He was still living inside it...

I tried explaining this to Maisie, but it just made her upset. She was still scared of that room, so I knew if I was going to go back, it would have to be alone. The staff might have locked the door, but they didn't lock the room where they kept the key, and it didn't take too much searching to find it. The next time our parents went away and left us with our grandmother, I was ready to explore again, to find my grandfather and meet him properly. He hadn't tried to hurt us, after all. He'd just stood up, and we'd gotten scared and ran away.

I stole the key, and hid it beneath my pillow. When night came, I waited until Maisie fell asleep, sneaking out of my room into the hall. My grandmother was watching television, facing away from the hall, and it was easy to creep past her and down the main stairwell of the house. I was walking barefoot, and the floor was icy cold on the bottom of my feet. Tip-toeing past boxes of new stock and inventory, I made my way down the corridor, eyes locked on the black door and the white ivory handle, shining like a beacon in the faint echoes of moonlight.

I'd taken a torch, but I didn't need it. As the door creaked open, an instinctive flick of the lightswitch revealed the staff had changed the broken lightbulbs before locking the door. The sudden, artificial light was almost blinding. The shrouded shapes were identical to my previous visit, though they weren't nearly as ominous without the shadows to ensnare them. It was reassuring, and the light made all my nerves vanish. More than ever, I was convinced - tonight I was going to meet my grandfather.

As I stalked between the sheet-covered shapes - somewhat familiar and recognisable from before - I noticed only one difference; the blocky shape of the sofa was vacant. Searching the last hidden spaces of the room, it quickly became obvious. My grandfather wasn't here. The room was empty, apart from the hidden treasures. A crushing weight settled over my shoulders, and I shook my head slightly, trying to ward off stinging tears. I was just a silly little girl, up past her bedtime chasing ghosts.

I walked back towards the sofa, wanting to sink down and go to sleep right there, but a hissing voice stopped me before I took my final steps.

"What are you doing?"

Maisie, at the doorway, rubbing sleep from her eyes.

I didn't see any point in lying. "I was looking for grandad. But he's not here. Nobody's here."

As if to check, Maisie's eyes drifted to the vacant sofa. I expected her to nod, and turn to leave, but instead, her eyes went wide and her lips began to tremble. She pointed, and I turned to look.

An insect, or something, was crawling beneath the dust sheet, right across the sofa cushions. It was the size of a small animal, like a rabbit, but the way the sheet moved was too spindly and angular. The sheet shifted and twisted around the shape of whatever was underneath. It could almost have been a spider, but each leg joint that poked under the sheet was as thick as my knuckle. If I'd have dared to move, I would have smashed it with my torch and kept hitting it until the dust sheet stopped moving.

Frozen as I was, all I could do was watch.

It crept forwards on the sofa, and as it went over the edge, it didn't fall. The sheets rippled, and it continued walking downwards, at the same, steady pace. Whatever it was, I'd soon find out. It was walking straight towards me, and was about to emerge from beneath the sheet.

The sheets wafted gently, as though stirred by a breeze, and something drifted out, elegant and smooth.

Fingers.

Clean, perfectly manicured fingers. A youthful woman's hand peeked out, each finger painted with red fingernail polish. The hand was so leisurely in its movements, floating above the ground, arm disappearing back beneath the sheets, yet there was no shape beyond the tautly draped fabric. There was nobody on the sofa. No way somebody could contort themselves to fit what little void existed between cloth and cushion.

I gawped, mouth unable to close as the hand slowly rotated and took hold of the sheet, raising higher and higher to reveal the floral patterned sofa and pinewood legs. As though it were a woman, hitching up her skirts. The colours of the sofa were so vivid and vibrant, it was hard to believe we hadn't noticed it before, even with a person distracting us, even in the near darkness. The flowers looked so real, you could almost see the morning dew forming on the petals, almost feel the sun's reflection glittering in the tilt of wind-brushed leaves. Before it rose above the cushioned seats, the hand released the dustsheet, and... beckoned me. It withdrew, slowly disappearing beneath the sheets, and the shape of the arm slithered away. The way it curved and twisted made me shiver. Even as young as I was, I knew no human arm could bend that way. Whatever was underneath that thin layer of fabric, it moved the way a snake did, writhing and uncoiling.

The sofa was dazzling. It appeared pure white behind the flowers. But it couldn't have been. It was too bright. 'White' somehow seemed... too dull a colour to describe it. It was almost blinding to look at, yet I couldn't stop myself. Maisie was at my side, and we both stared unblinking at the fabric and flowers and this new colour our eyes had never seen before. Birds fluttered into the room, with silent flapping wings. Hummingbirds. Dozens of them, hovering and sipping from the flowers of the fabric. It took me a long moment to realise they weren't in the room at all. They were just another pattern, stitched into the fabric of the cushion. And yet they were... moving. One by one, they zipped beneath the covering, following the hand. And for a moment, I wanted to follow them. I took a step forward and stopped myself. Maisie had made the same step forwards. At the exact same time. We turned to look at each other, peeling our eyes away from the sofa.

That was enough. Something deep and primal told me I shouldn't sit down, yet somehow it was easier to stop each other than stop ourselves. We didn't speak, but together, my sister and I left the room, gripping hold of each other and never breaking eye contact. When we reached the door, I flicked off the light and shut the creaking door with all my strength. As the room with the ivory handle vanished from view, I saw for one, brief moment, a man. He was barely visible in the darkness, but he sat on the sofa, hands on his knees. His cold eyes met mine, and even the half second before the door closed was too long. The moment the door was shut, I locked it.

We never went into that room again. Neither me or Maisie have ever spoken about it. To each other, or anyone else. She might not even remember. Perhaps I would have been able to dismiss it as childish fantasy, if it wasn't for the thing I saw yesterday.

My grandmother passed away last year. Her ashes were kept in an urn, but during the house sale and all the moving, somehow the ashes... got lost. They found the urn, which never left the house. But the ashes were gone.

Obviously my family was devastated. A few people who probably didn't deserve it got fired, but we never found out who was responsible, or what happened.

During the final weeks of the house sale, all of our grandfather's vast fortune and old treasures got divided amongst family, friends and loyal employees. Without doubt, the most highly desired artifacts were locked behind a large door with an ivory handle. Maisie and myself avoided that particular day of exploration.

But as I said my last goodbyes to the house, I couldn't help but notice a familiar shape amongst the others, draped beneath dust sheets. The blocky outline of a sofa, with something placed atop it. Something with a head, and shoulders. The vague outline of a person, perched on the sofa with room to spare. At the very bottom, peeking beneath the sheets was the trim of a faded, green dress, and matching green buckled shoes.

My grandmother's shoes.

Whatever was wearing them shifted slightly beneath the dust sheet, turning to face me.

And patted the empty seat.

**Item 042**
**"TWO-SEATER"**

[purchased by Ministry Personnel at auction]

# Item 042

Pool balls split across the table with a satisfying crack. Tom Nelly lined up his cue and potted ball after ball, not caring whether they were stripes or spots. He just pocketed the easiest shot available, or otherwise just hit something as hard as he could, until the table was as empty as the guard quarters themselves. Laying the cue back on the table, Tom sighed and stretched his back muscles.

*Where the hell is everyone*, he wondered, glancing around the room as though someone might be hiding behind the furniture. His hand lingered on the plastic triangle under the pool table, but Tom couldn't bring himself to rack up the balls again just to play by himself. Some of the guards, Tom knew, would be on shift. And he supposed, looking at the time, that it would be handover right about now. One group wrapping up their patrols, another group just commencing. Shift leaders would meet up and discuss any issues, and then they'd switch. But there should still be plenty of other guards on rest or standby, like Tom was.

He hadn't been working on Floor Fifty-Four long enough to know if this was out of the ordinary, but this was the first time he'd seen the guard quarters without a single person lounging around, goofing off or fast asleep. The silence and the boredom was driving him crazy. Shaking his head, he began putting on his uniform. Somehow, Tom was so bored that he was about to spend his first day off patrolling the halls - just to find out where everyone was.

His first guess was to try the outposts. These were small breakrooms dotted around Floor Fifty-Four where the guards could rest without having to traipse all the way back to quarters. Some of these were nicer than others. Outpost A - affectionately called 'The Angel' due to an item you had to pass en route - had been made up to look like a local pub, and was Tom's personal favourite. It was also where most of the guards were likely to be hanging out, given that it had two large refrigerators stuffed full of beers.

With boots laced up and armour padding strapped on top of his uniform, Tom's hand lingered over the rest of his equipment. He shouldn't need it. The only reason he was wearing the uniform was to avoid reprimand - he could hardly skulk about the hall in his civvies. Yet he found himself clutching his baton and strapping it in place on his belt all the same. It was strange really. He knew it wouldn't do him any good against most of the objects and creatures inside these walls, but he couldn't let himself walk around without at least some form of defence. Comforted by the reassuring weight of his weapon, Tom shut his locker and headed outside into the maze of corridors.

There were probably more direct routes to the Outpost, but Tom kept to his patrol route. The last thing he needed was to get lost. He tried to ignore the strange objects he walked past, but some of them caught his eye. Especially the ones that... moved.

A little toy train ran in tight little circles inside its cell, until Tom walked past. Then its wooden train tracks broke away and began climbing the glass, as though an invisible hand was laying them down. The train followed at a crawl, matching Tom's pace. Just before he stepped out of sight, the tracks veered off at wild angles, the train cutting an impossible, jerky zig-zag. As though it was furious it couldn't reach him.

One particularly large cell filled with plump cushions and pet toys made Tom jump out of his skin when a fuzzy black and white cat leapt out of thin air to land at its centre. Tom had always thought this cell was empty. The cat clutched something in its mouth, some small animal. Whatever it was, Tom had never seen one before in his life. Not quite a mouse, not quite a frog. Tom couldn't think of any animal that was such a violent shade of electric blue. Now Tom looked closer, the cat didn't have fur at all. It glowed with fuzzy static that TV screens used to show when they had no signal. The static cat arched its back and stretched out its paws, softly illuminating its cell.

Although the corridor continued straight on, and though Tom was certain it led to the Outpost he was heading to, he stuck like glue to his usual patrol route. It took him down a horseshoe with several rooms jutting off. Each room was filled to bursting with paper, neatly stacked on shelves that climbed to the ceiling. The shelves were numbered, but Tom couldn't make sense of it. There didn't seem to be any logical order. Still, there were technicians in white coats inside some of these rooms, looking at individual pages and scratching their heads. As he made his way to the centre of the horseshoe, Tom paused, watching the fax machine at its centre. It printed out page, after page, after page. Endlessly. They fell to the floor, one atop the other.

"Morning," Tom said, as a technician exited one of the storage rooms and scanned his hand to gain access to the cell with the fax machine.

"Is it?" replied the technician, heading inside and scooping up the papers off the floor. After piling them up as neatly as he could, he ripped open a fresh ream of paper and began topping up the fax machine.

Shrugging, Tom carried on his route, exiting the horseshoe corridor. He'd been right; this just lead out back into the same hallway as before. He could have missed that out entirely. *Better safe than sorry,* Tom told himself.

At a junction which lead to the Angel, Tom overheard the clamour of gruff voices echoing from a different direction. He paused, listening intently. Definitely male voices, loud and careless. There was a peel of laughter that made Tom's decision easy - the eggheads never laughed. Veering off into the unknown for the first time, Tom headed toward the voices.

It didn't take long to reach the cluster of guards, all gathered around one cell, blocking it from Tom's sight. As his footsteps drew him closer, the incoherent tangle of voices became clearer.

"Yer full of shit, Bryce."

"Why would I make it up? Honest to God, she was right there! Duggie saw her, didn't you Duggie?"

"Aye."

"See?"

"Bollocks, you've slipped him some cash. Duggie would say owt for a fiver. Wouldn't you Duggie?"

"...Aye."

None of them noticed as Tom stepped closer. There was six guards huddled around the glass, pressed in so tight that Tom had to stand on tip-toes to see what was inside. This cell was dark, the lights dimmed so much it made it hard to make out the sofa inside. The harsh lighting from the corridor didn't help. If it wasn't for the white cushions, Tom probably wouldn't have been able to see it at all.

Bryce reeled on Duggie. "Whose side are you on?" he spat with exasperation.

"He's right though," Duggie admitted in a thick Aberdeen accent, "I did see the lass."

One of the accusing guards leaned in close, lowering his voice to a conspiratorial murmur. "Know what I reckon?"

The other guards began to grin wider, until they looked like a pack of Cheshire cats.

"I reckon these two are so starved of some fanny," continued the accuser, "they saw that old grandma and got all hot and bothered."

The guards erupted. Even Duggie burst out laughing at that. Tom caught himself smiling, even though he didn't get the joke. Bryce shook his head like a cornered bull. "Last time I show you lot. Bunch of pricks."

"Come on Bryce," chimed in another. "You think we're gonna believe you saw some stunning blonde bird in her knickers, just sat here waiting for you?"

"I can believe the blonde," said one. "It's the 'waiting for you' bit I'm struggling with..."

Another round of laughs made Bryce's ears flush red. He raised his meaty fist and levelled a finger at the one who'd caused the laughter. "I'm not a liar. We'll try this again, shall we?"

With that, Bryce looked away, staring intently down the far end of the corridor. The other guards rolled their eyes, and then did something similar, all staring off in random directions at something Tom couldn't see. Glancing around and wondering where to look, Tom's eyes fell upon the sofa at the centre of the cell. With all the others preoccupied, he could finally get a good look at the thing. It sat on timber feet, and had floral patterned cushions. Even in the darkness, it looked grubby.

All of the guards snapped their heads back at the same time to share Tom's view. It was so unexpected that Tom almost gasped out loud.

"Nothing," Bryce said, before abruptly looking away again. The other guards did the same.

Bemused, Tom resumed his study of the sofa. He wasn't sure what the others were expecting to happen, but barely a second had passed before they did the same thing again, all twisting their heads to stare at the sofa.

"Nothing," Bryce repeated.

As they began to turn their heads away a third time, Duggie spotted Tom and pointed at him. "Tha's why! He's not looking away!"

Everyone turned to look at Tom, blinking in surprise at his presence.

"New lad!" spat Bryce, prodding a finger at Tom's chest hard enough to be felt through kevlar. "No wonder she's not showing. Christ sake."

Offering a bemused shrug, Tom flinched as his head was gripped tight between Bryce's fingers, forcing him to turn away and stare down the corridor.

"Right, nobody look," snarled Bryce, going as far as clamping his eyes shut.

Reluctantly, Tom did the same. Apparently it wasn't good enough, because a moment later, Bryce let out a groan. When Tom opened his eyes and turned back to the sofa, his stomach did a death roll. Where before, there had just been an empty sofa, there was now a strange man, sat on the cushions, enveloped in the shadows of the room. Despite the darkness, Tom could make out the immaculate suit, all blacks and whites, to match his slicked back hair and pasty skin. As though he'd stepped out of an old photograph, before they invented colour. His hawkish eyes - crushed beneath a stern and hateful brow - were locked on Tom.

"You're ballsing this all up, Newbie," muttered Bryce, shaking his head. "Look away..."

"Wh-who is he?" Tom stammered, unable to peel his gaze away from the stranger. The man had his hands placed atop both knees, and did nothing except stare, his chest slowly rising and falling the only sign he was alive at all.

"Look away!" insisted Bryce, reaching out for Tom's skull once more, but Tom twisted out of reach and turned away before he could. Barely a second passed before Bryce spoke again, bitter disappointment on his tongue.

"Nothing..."

When Tom looked back, the strange man was gone. The sofa was completely empty again, nothing else inside the cell at all. To the rest of the guards, whatever disappearing act had taken place was business as usual, and without saying a word they turned away again.

They repeated this. Over... and over... and over. All the guards would look away, and the sofa would either be empty, or some strange person would be sat atop its plump, floral cushions. Tom couldn't understand how they could appear so quickly. Practically in the blink of an eye. As this strange ritual of looking away and looking back continued, Tom would try to catch them out, twisting back as quickly as he could in hopes he'd see one climbing out from behind the sofa, or under it, or from inside the cushions. Anything, really. Any logical explanation would be better than the alternative.

"Are they... ghosts?" Tom asked, watching the latest appearance - an elderly woman in a green dress - beckon him over, gently patting the seat next to her.

“Nah,” said one guard. “They’re physical, Duggie tried throwing coins at one to see if it was a ghost, and the coins just bounced right off. Like it was a normal person, you know? We’re not supposed to get too close, apparently they’ll try and grab you.”

Tom did his best not to shiver. Inside Cell 042, the old lady pointed at him, becoming more insistent with her gestures to join her. Her wrinkled lips twisted into a pleasant motherly smile. Worst of all, there was some small part of Tom’s brain telling him it was OK. *She’s just a nice old lady. And those seats do look comfortable.* For a moment he could imagine how nice it would feel to rest his feet, and sink down into the fabric.

He shook himself. Everyone else had turned away, and were waiting for him to do the same. When Tom looked back, the old lady had vanished. In her place, a grungy looking tramp lay sprawled out across both seats, fast asleep. He’d shown up a few times. Each time he did the same routine, jolting awake and casting a bemused expression at his audience.

“Well...” one of the guards sneered at Bryce, “as fun as this has been... I can think of better ways to spend my day off.”

There were murmurs of agreement from the others. Even Duggie was yawning. Bryce spat out obscene objections, cursing the lot of them and insisting his fantasy girl would show up if they just kept looking.

The tramp inside Cell 042 had pushed himself into a seated position now, running a grimy hand through what remained of his hair. He flashed a sheepish grin at Tom, all stained teeth and gums. He made an expansive gesture that took in all the guards, and motioned to the empty seat next to him, as if to say “there’s plenty of room”. None of them spoke, Tom had noticed. Not that he’d have been able to hear them through the reinforced glass, but their lips never moved. They all just gesticulated with their hands and facial expressions. Every single one of them encouraging Tom to sit down next to them.

Tom only stirred when one of the other guards nudged into him as they left, walking back down the corridor. Bryce stayed for a moment, looking back and forth, back and forth, trying to will his mystery woman into existence. Tom played along, still intrigued by the sofa and its visitors.

But when nobody showed up except for the tramp, over and over, even Bryce gave up hope. He pounded a fist against the glass and turned on his heels, growling to himself. As a parting gift, he shouldered Tom out of the way. Tom almost muttered something under his breath, but bit his tongue at the last moment. It was still far too soon for that. He'd need some friends down here before he starting picking fights.

Tom settled for a middle finger, aimed squarely at Bryce's back as he stormed off, looking ready to punch the next person he saw. *The others were right,* Tom thought, *this is a waste of time.*

As he began to walk back to the guard's quarters himself, he gave one last considering glance at the sofa in Cell 042. And stopped dead in his tracks.

Perched on the dimly lit cushions was the most beautiful woman Tom had ever seen. Shrouded in shadows, she idly twirled a finger through luscious blonde curls that glimmered in the darkness. Her other hand rested on her bare, naked thigh, one thumb looped under the elastic lining of her underwear - sleek, satin, white. Maryln Monroe flashed to the forefront of Tom's mind. This girl - this woman - was a dead ringer. Ample curves in every place a red blooded man could dream. All the while, she watched him with an intensity that made Tom's cheeks grow hot.

She must have noticed, because she smiled. The slightest curve of her lips, almost a smirk, deepening the dimples on her cheeks. Even the way she blinked felt intentional, a slow flutter of her eyelashes that made him want to melt. Tom didn't realise how close he had stepped forwards until he felt cold glass beneath his fingers. He stepped away, shaking himself out of his trance to the best of his abilities.
"Guys..." he croaked. Or tried to. His mouth moved, but only dry air came out.

The woman on the sofa tilted her head, arching her back ever so slightly to exaggerate the slopes of her body. The way the light danced across her skin silenced all thoughts of calling for the others. She wanted him. Tom could tell. An unspoken language that only the eyes could speak. And there was no doubt in Tom's mind that he wanted her right back. Vague ideas of all the things he wanted to do with her floated to his mind, and began to swell, replacing any rational part of his mind.

How long since he'd been with a woman in that way now? Over a year, at least. Tom had never been good with relationships, or girls in general, and joining the army hadn't helped that.

It wouldn't hurt to get a little closer, would it? This hallway was so bright, Tom's reflection on the glass was more vivid than the woman inside. If he just stepped inside the cell, he'd have a much clearer view. Maybe he could even talk to her. Hear her voice.

Without even thinking about it, Tom's hand had lifted to the access panel. Not scanning his palm for entry, just resting on it, bracing himself for support. Like his body was showing him exactly where it wanted to go. The scanner glowed with soft, inviting light, his hand lingering above. On his first day at Floor Fifty-Four, the head of security had told Tom to never enter a cell without knowing the rules first. But the others said Duggie had been close enough to throw things at the people on the sofa. He must have been inside the cell to do that. That part must be safe, at least...

Drawing her knees up to her breasts, the woman inside Cell 042 nestled herself deeper into the sofa. With slow, deliberate movements, she swung her feet over the armrest, until her calves hung lazily over the edge. Then she lay down, running fingertips across her toned stomach. All the while, her hungry eyes locked with Tom's. Batting her eyelids closed in self-indulgent bliss, she bit her lip and moved her fingertips lower, and lower, and lower.

Catching himself on raised tip-toes, Tom promptly brought himself back down to earth and followed it with the driest swallow of his life. His nose had been pressed against the glass. The animal part of his mind had grasped the human part in a vice grip, and every atom of his manhood wanted to step inside this room, be closer to this woman. Puffing out his cheeks in sheer exasperation, he released a long held breath, before curling his hand into a fist and bumping it repeatedly over the scanner.

He couldn't go inside. He was specifically told not to go inside. He really, really, shouldn't go inside.

Tom glanced across his shoulder, down the corridor to his left. Completely empty. He did the same to his other side, confirming he was completely alone. He closed his eyes, shaking his head like a spooked horse. Hating himself more than a little bit, Tom kept his eyes clamped shut as he felt blindly for the scanner and place his palm at the centre.

There was a melodic beep, and a hydraulic hiss. Tom opened his eyes as the door swung open.

Nobody was there. Just the empty sofa, sat in the centre of the cell, reminding Tom how much of a fool he had just been. So desperate for female attention that he opened this containment cell, risked his life, and other people's, for what? A better look at a woman who didn't even exist?

"Shit," Tom hissed under his breath, as a blockade of sexual chemicals tumbled down in an instant and the full weight of his mistake flooded through his mind like a broken dam. "Shit, Shit, Shit! Idiot. You stupid idiot!"

Shooting nervous glances across each shoulder down both ends of the corridor, Tom slapped his palm back on the scanner, desperately willing the door shut. The hiss it made as it closed sounded like mocking laughter to Tom's ears.

Breathing a sign of relief as the door to Cell 042 sealed shut, Tom thumped a fist against his own forehead in frustration at his own foolishness. As he turned to trudge down the corridor, he shook his head. All he could think was how glad he was that nobody had seen him do that.

Inside Cell 042, The Narrator burst out laughing, spraying biscuit crumbs across the room. He held up both hands apologetically. "Terribly sorry, these stories just tickle me sometimes..." Chuckling to himself, he repeated the last line of the latest chapter he'd been reading again under his breath, "*'nobody had seen him...'* Aaah, they really have no idea, do they?"

He snapped the book shut, and wafted it aloft. On the cover, glinting in what little light reached it, the title read 'The life of Tom Nelly'.

"I wouldn't get too attached..." mused The Narrator, examining the cover himself. "It's a very short book." One of The Narrator's fingers remained wedged between the pages, holding his place in the story. "Not many pages left..." He casually thumbed through what remained before the hardcover back, stopping on the final white page. "Hmmm. He dies in this very room..."

Gazing around Cell 042 with mild interest, The Narrator took in the walls, the little camera mounted above him, the sofa and the beautiful blonde woman on its cushions. He peered over his armrest as if there might be something untoward beneath his chair. "I can't imagine how. Can you?" he asked the blonde.

She didn't reply. She didn't seem to notice him at all.

Stifling a yawn and stuffing 'The life of Tom Nelly' back into his bookshelf, The Narrator shook his head, thumbing dismissively in the direction of the woman on the sofa. "Dull as dishwater, this one. Never has anything interesting to say."

Adjusting in his chair, The Narrator ran his hands down both the armrests. "Plus, I can't help but feel we start looking like a living room when we're together."

The bookshelf at the side of him became so filled with books that it began to violently shudder. More and more appeared into existence on the top shelf, pressing into those adjacent, becoming tighter and tighter. They began to strain outwards, spines bulging out. The Narrator held up a hand just as the pressure became too much and one book was forced out, flying into the air like a freshly popped champagne cork, landing snugly into his outstretched fingers. The other books seemed to settle down at this, content with surrendering one of their own. Without missing a beat, The Narrator flicked open the pages of this latest tome and began to read.

"But still, she's been here a long time. Practically part of the furniture..." He smiled to himself at his own joke, but the more he read the book in his hands, the more grave his expression grew. "But not everything on Floor Fifty-Four fits in so nicely."

"No. Some things are not of this world," The Narrator sighed to himself. "No matter how much they want to be."

# “Apollo 17”

*[ posted on internet forum by potential witness ]*

Everyone knows Apollo 11.

I was barely more than a boy, but I still remember it vividly. Neil Armstrong, descending the ladder. The words ‘LIVE FROM THE MOON’ emblazoned across our tiny black and white television. My mother, telling me over and over that I was sitting “too darn close!”

Everyone watched the launch, and the landing itself, but I watched the whole thing. Even thinking about it now after all these years gives me goosebumps. Man on the moon. I’ll say it again for the kids on the back row - man on the goddamn moon! When Neil said those famous, beautiful words... I’m not ashamed to say I cried, in fact I was proud. Proud to be American. Proud to be a human being. What else could we achieve? What was the ceiling of our potential? That one defining moment is to thank for my entire career. For my love of science fiction. For all the hope that I hold in my heart for the human race.

So yes, everyone knows Apollo 11.

But not many people know Apollo 17. 1972. The last man on the moon.

It’s a mission I know quite a lot about, considering I helped run it. It was a few years on from the first landing, and I was a wet behind the ears technician, supervising the flight director. My first mission, actually, and without doubt my most memorable.

I’ll pause here. All my life I’ve done what I was ordered to. I never told a soul about what we saw that day. Not to my parents, rest their souls. Not even to my wife. Even if integrity wasn't at stake, we knew this wasn't a standard NDA. Breaking this wouldn't be some lawsuit and a slap on the wrist - I had friends go missing.

So I kept schtum. I've followed orders all my life, and this was no exception. But, it's funny how feelings can change when we get close to the end. Me and Sandra never had kids, though lord knows we had fun trying. She was my world, and my rock. I feel lucky to have even met her, nevermind married her. Last year she passed away, and it kind of felt like I was done. Life decided to emphasise that point, and two months ago I found out I had the big C followed by the t-word that nobody wants to hear next. I've come to terms with it, if I'm honest. I've got no family to leave anything to, just this secret that's burning a hole in my soul. If I'd had children, perhaps I'd whisper it to them. Maybe it's that little bit of hope inside me, but I feel like people need to know.

There's a reason we never went back.

I know someone who tried to speak out before. He put it on a conspiracy theory forum, apparently. I figure they have people looking on there, scanning for keywords and the like. That's why I'm posting here. Maybe they don't track fiction with the same filters, on account of all these stories setting them off non stop. Maybe I'm wrong, and maybe they'll kill me. But as I said, I'm kind of finished anyway, so here goes nothing.

Apollo 17 was primarily a geological and scientific venture. We'd mastered the art of launching a tin can filled with spacemen by this point, and wanted to learn as much as we could about this new frontier that had only been in our grasp for three years. That meant samples; lots and lots of samples.

Taken from as many different locations as we could manage in the alloted time that the harsh conditions and our technological limitations allowed. We set multiple records actually. Longest time spent on the Moon (three days), longest vehicular trip on the surface, largest rock samples gathered, most lunar orbits (seventy five), longest time spent in lunar orbit. As you can see, duration and scale were the name of the game.

Three astronauts went up with the shuttle, but only two travelled to the surface with the lunar lander. One man has to watch his dreams completed from afar. Close but no cigar, as they say. The two men who would be the last to set foot on our closest heavenly body were Eugene Cernan and Harrison Schmitt. Nice guys, it has to be said.

The first moonwalk took place within hours of touching down at the landing site. There was an immediate screw-up when the rear fender of the Lunar Rover (also called an LVR or, if you're completely dimwitted, a Moon buggy) broke during offloading. That's American engineering for you - can get you to the Moon, but the mud guards of your go-kart will fall right off. Might seem like a small problem, but without the mud guards, all that dust is going to kick up right over you and your spacesuit. You know, the pressurised suit keeping you alive. That suit.

So the crew on the Moon, in space and back on Earth put our heads together and devised a method of repair using the most advanced technology available. We used duct tape. This worked for a while, but the duct tape kept getting covered with lunar dust the moment it peeled from the reel, which drastically reduced its adhesiveness. As such, the fender kept falling off. This would be mildly annoying on a bike ride, nevermind on a cold, dead rock in the middle of space. The first day ended, and whilst the crew slept in their lunar lander, we tried to create a prototype fender using materials we knew the guys had available. After an all nighter and much head banging, we came up with the solution. We used duct tape again. But this time, we used it inside the lunar lander (no lunar dust in there) making a new makeshift fender, and clamping it back on.

As such, day two was a tremendous success. Without having to offload the LVR and track back to pick up the mudguard every half hour, Eugene and Harrison made astonishing progress, surpassing all expectations we had for the quantity and diversity of samples. By the end of the second day, we had reached our best estimate of samples for the journey, and still had a day in hand. The hope was that without having to spend the morning constructing a makeshift fender or offloading equipment, it might be possible to travel to even further reaches on the surface and collect samples we'd originally had to remove from the scope of the mission.

We had cameras mounted to the LVR, which had a slight delay; around five seconds. There were also cameras that could be carried and operated by the crew, but we'd carried out all our initial shots and footage on day one, wanting to focus the rest of the mission on scientific discovery rather than documentation. Much of day three went without incident, but as the crew travelled to a valley which we believed would contain materials from impact craters, we noticed a blip on the cameras.

Eugene and Harrison had disembarked, then a moment later, the screen must have jumped back, because Harrison walked past the buggy again. I flagged it up as a camera glitch and thought nothing else of it.

One thing you have to understand is that expeditions are

long. Very long. All day meticulously pouring over data, the camera screens almost become a luxury. A vanity. We mostly ignore them. The numbers are more important. That's the only explanation I can give for why it took us so long to notice.

"Is Ronald with them?"

To this day, I don't know whose voice it was. I just remember the way it sounded. Confused, afraid, hopeful. As if the words themselves were saying 'please'.

All eyes turned to the screens above us. At the astronauts. One. Two. Three.

You might have heard loud noises in your life. I promise you no sound is louder than mission command falling deathly silent.

Three astronauts.

I don't know how long we watched that screen. I couldn't look away. Eugene and Harrison, collecting rock samples from the ground. Just behind them, another astronaut, stood patiently watching.

My supervising flight director spoke first. He grabbed the comms module and spoke in a calm, flat voice that felt like spiders crawling along my spine.

"Eugene, Harrison, this is command, we need you to return to the lander."

I didn't dare breathe as I watched the two men continue to lethargically collect rocks, low gravity making them look infinitely slow. There was still that delay to factor in too. I tried to estimate the distance between the figures. Twenty metres, maybe fifteen? Eugene's voice came over the comms before the video showed him raise his hand to radio in.

"Sure thing command, we'll wrap up here then-"

"We need you to return to the lander please."

There was a pause as the Astronauts digested this. My director jumped in before they could raise further protests.

"Situation has changed, we need you to return immediately."

Command was slowly waking up now, people were moving. Telephones were ringing. We had prepared for every situation imaginable. Crashes. Launch failures. One astronaut dying. Both astronauts dying. All astronauts abandoned. But an additional astronaut, of unknown origin? No. No, we hadn't planned for that.

We heard a panicked cry. On the video feed, Eugene and Harrison had turned to look at each other, and Harrison had seen the strange addition. He flinched backwards, lifting off the ground and stumbling in slow motion. Eugene saw him too.

"What th-"

"We need you to return to the lander immediately."

"Command, who is that?"

"Return to the lander."

"Command, wh- who - Ron? Is that you?"

"Return to the fucking lander!"

Harrison was scrambling amongst the dust, Eugene stepping backwards. The third figure just watched, black screened helmet turning as it followed them. We could hear frantic breathing. Comms that had carried vital information now just recorded the simple sounds of two men running, fighting their way through thick black soup in spacesuits. The camera feed - how many nightmares I've had of that camera feed - showed them trying their best, bouncing around, dust everywhere, clawing their way across the surface. Behind them, the third figure just stood perfectly still.

They made it to the LVR, one astronaut to each side of the

screen, this stranger stood between them in the distance. Their breathing was still laboured over the comms, but you could hear the shift. The hesitation. We had the same moment at mission control. We were people who demanded answers. We were people who would literally go to the moon to get them. What in the name of God was this third person doing there?

My flight director made the call. It was the call we all knew was right, but none of us truly wanted.

"Return. To. The. Lander."

There were a few considering breaths before Eugene's voice came through.

"Yeah. Yeah, OK."

Then Harrison began shouting.

"Oh fuck, go go go!"

Our eyes drifted to the screen, the images still with their slight delay. The moment the LVR began to shift into reverse, the third astronaut began to move. Not the slow, methodic bounces of a moonwalk, but that same frantic scramble Eugene and Harrison had made to escape. As though it was copying them. As though it thought that was the way people always moved. An astronaut doesn't move quickly. Whoever was inside wouldn't be able to punch or strike with any real speed or damage in low gravity. It couldn't get me through the screen. And yet I have never felt fear like I did in that room at that moment.

The lunar surface reeled as Eugene turned the LVR, dust kicking up and masking the camera. We couldn't see behind them, only directly in front. The LVR is never operated at full speed, best practise is to take it nice and steady. It got a full performance test on day three. It was a long, horrible drive that took two hours.

In that time, as I wasn't prepping for the launch, I poured over the footage. A few people were arguing it must be a secret space program, from another nation - most likely Russia. The suit looked American, but perhaps it had been done that way on purpose. I just remembered the way it ran. It didn't move like a trained astronaut. It didn't move like a person at all. It moved like something pretending to be human and getting it wrong. Earlier, I'd flagged up a camera glitch. That let me easily find the first frame where the third astronaut had appeared. It wasn't a camera glitch at all. The thing had been following them for twenty minutes.

Loading and unloading the LVR takes around half an hour, if you're doing it properly. We abandoned it on the surface. Eugene and Harrison ran straight onto the lunar lander and we carried out the fastest launch procedure ever performed (another record, albeit unrecorded).

There were additional cameras, watching the engines. These ignited, spitting fire out and blasting the lander back into space, back towards the command module. I know I wasn't the only one to get one last glimpse though. As the rocket lifted off the ground, the camera caught a wider angle of the surface.

For just a moment, you could make out a solitary astronaut. Looking up. Watching us leave.

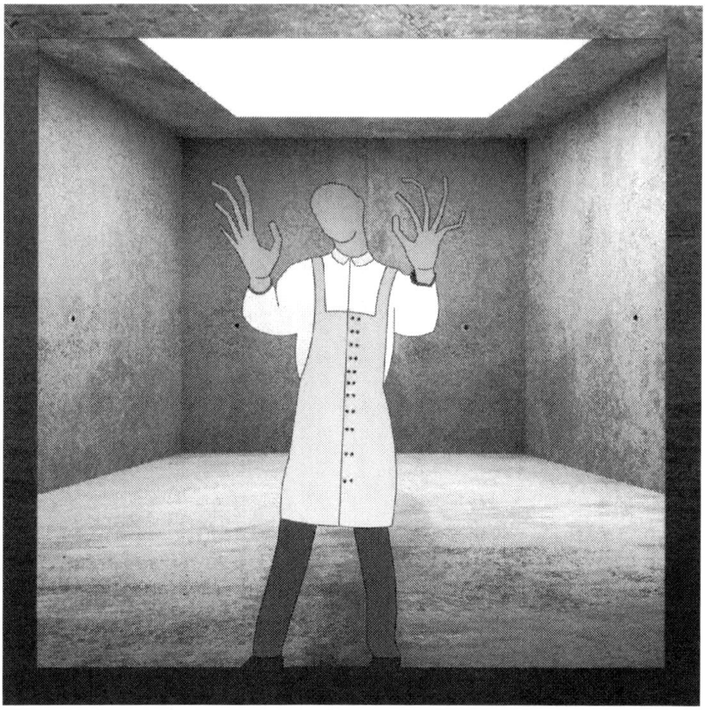

## Item 210
## "COPYCAT"

[relocated from Floor Thirty]

# Item 210

"We got this one off the Yanks," said Paul Slater, his voice stained with the century-old soot of London Town. Head of Security at Floor Fifty-Four, Paul was a big man. A permanent frown seemed carved into his stone-like face, deep wrinkles prominent even against his dark complexion. There was more stubble on his jaw than the top of his head, shaved buzz-cut-short to hide any accusations of approaching baldness. Not that anyone would dare mention it to his face.

"They used to keep it on Floor Thirty with the rest of the monsters, but didn't take them long to decide that was the big daddy of shit ideas, so we got lumped with it."

The young man at Paul's side shook his head. "Monsters," muttered Tom Nelly, "don't think I'll ever get used to this place."

Paul stepped up to the entrance of Wing 210 and let it scan his retina. "You will," he said, not a trace of reassurance in his voice, just plain matter-of-fact. Green light and a sharp buzzing alarm welcomed Paul Slater, the double doors sliding apart to grant him access. He was striding through them before they'd finished moving. Tom scurried in after him.

Their heavy boots marched on the concrete floor, the cells to either side of them completely empty, interior lights on low. Tom's eyes searched them all, quick glances from the corners of his eyes. The only thing moving quicker than his eyes were his feet, ensnared in some primal need to rejoin the bigger, more confident man ahead.

When Tom finally caught up, Paul held out a meaty paw and stopped him. A baton snapped into Paul's hand, and he pointed at a thick red line on the floor. "Remember what these mean?"

"Yeah," said Tom, "I remember. From the induction."

Paul turned his gaze to the young man. "Go on then."

"It means danger. If we pass over that line, this thing can affect us."

Paul nodded slowly. "So what are you gonna do now?"

"Err..." Tom scratched his head. "Find out what kind of danger?"

With a curt bow of his head, Paul reached into his top pocket and pulled out a neatly folded slip of paper, before handing it to Tom. The moment the paper left Paul's fingers, he set a timer on his watch, then resumed his march down the corridor.

Tom unfolded the paper, revealing a bullet pointed safety briefing and a cartoon infographic with a little figure inside a box. Another version of the same figure was also outside the box with an exclamation mark above its head.

*Item 210 - "Copycat"*
*WHAT YOU NEED TO KNOW*

* *This item may copy your appearance*
* *It can only do this when you are close to it*
* *Do not stay within Wing 210 for longer than fifteen minutes*
* *Wait at least eight hours before returning*
* *If item has eyes, leave Wing 210 immediately and inform your superior*
* *If cell is empty, leave Wing 210 immediately and inform your*

*superior*
** DO NOT ENTER CELL FOR ANY REASON, AT ANY TIME, EVER*

Tom gave it a quick skim before running after Paul's hulking figure. He began to ask a question, though even as the words left his lips, he wasn't entirely sure what he even wanted to ask.

Paul interrupted him regardless. "There's one of those for each item. If you're entering a cell, any area with a number, or passing a red line, make sure you've read it."

Tom decided on his question. "What happens if we stay longer than fifteen minutes?"

"Don't know. Don't want to. Make sure you're not the reason I find out."

Tom swallowed and gave another read of the slip of paper. It didn't seem like Paul Slater was the kind of man you wanted to upset on your first day, nor did Floor Fifty-Four seem the place where you wanted to make mistakes, ever. After a moment though, Paul stopped moving, turning towards one of the cells. Tom looked up from the safety briefing. The cell they had stopped at was the only one on Wing 210 that wasn't empty.

Behind reinforced glass was a figure without a face. It stood proudly, its spine oddly straight, its hands pressed against the glass. It was wearing a guard's uniform, was the same height and build as Tom Nelly, and its featureless head was pointing right at him.

"Thought it would go for you," said Paul conversationally, "it likes new shapes."

Tom stared at the thing inside the cell. It *did* look like him, or at least the basic shape of him. It didn't have ears, eyes, nose or a mouth. Instead of hair, its flesh was just a different colour, smeared over the top of its skull. Assuming it had a skull. It looked as though it did, with skin stretched tight around it. Now Tom looked closer, the uniform was the same as the hair, just colour staining its skin. But as he watched, it seemed to bulge at the shoulders, elbows and knees. Bony joints swelled, starting to look more like the protective pads that Tom himself wore. Its feet were swelling too, forming heavy black boots.

Perhaps instinctively, Tom took a step back. That just made the thing lean closer, pressing its empty face into the glass. Its fingers splayed unnaturally wide, unnaturally long. Its whole body pressed into the glass now, and Tom could almost feel its desire to press into him, to merge with him.

“It just copies your appearance first,” said Paul, tapping the glass lightly with his baton. The creature’s head turned to him briefly, and its skin momentarily grew slightly darker, its whole body swelling ever so slightly to copy Paul’s larger frame. But then its head snapped back to Tom, and it resumed its slow refinement of his figure. On the top of its head, thin fibers slowly spread out, like a thousand spiders lifting their legs. An imitation of Tom’s hair.

“Then it copies your behaviour. It’ll speak your voice. Share your memories. Know everything you know. And once it’s figured that out, once it’s become a perfect copy, it’ll try to replace you.”

Tom didn’t even try to suppress the shiver that slithered down his spine. “It can’t do that though, can it? From behind the glass?”

As if in response, Copycat snatched back its hands and tremors shook its whole body. Impersonating the shiver that had just taken hold of Tom.

"They don't think so. But they don't know for sure. Management won't let them test that far." Paul tapped on the glass again, but this time the creature ignored him. Its uniform no longer looked like flesh, and had stopped swelling. With each passing second, its texture seemed to be more refined, and Tom felt like he was looking into a steamy mirror that was beginning to clear. Tom almost forgot Paul was there, and jumped when he spoke again. "Once it has a shape, it can hold it for days, and switch back to it, quickly. It doesn't just copy memories, either. It can copy abilities. That's why they took it out of Floor Thirty."

Tom shook his head. "Isn't that the best place for it though? If they can keep the other monsters there, why does it matter?"

"Because one day they found it in the halls," said Paul. He almost sounded bored. "They didn't even realise until it turned into something else. Thought it was just a normal escape."

Tom actually laughed at that. "Just a normal monster escape..." he muttered.

Behind the glass, the figure silently tilted its head back and shook its shoulders. Loose strands of hair fell from its head. Its uniform had stitching now, and text. Its hands had fingernails instead of flesh on both sides.

"They're prepared for escapes. Strobe lights and gas grenades will bring a vampire to its knees, but won't do much if that same vampire then turns into a golem, or a werewolf, or a siren, or... you get the idea. Without realising what they were doing, they'd accidentally made a swiss-fucking-army knife of monsters. The only reason they caught it was because it couldn't impersonate a guard, at least not quickly enough. So now we don't give it chance. Fifteen minutes. No more." As he said it, Paul lifted his arm and glanced at his watch.

Tom realised his jaw was open and snapped it shut. "So why even visit it? Why not leave it alone?"

"I start every shift here," said Paul, stepping up to the glass, getting in between Tom and his mirror image. "I like to make sure it's still here. Still blank."

He turned and motioned for Tom to follow as he continued down the corridor. Tom gave one last look at Copycat, and even though it had no eyes, there was no denying it stared right back. Its face had defined ridges now, a nose without nostrils. Lips without a mouth. Eye sockets, covered with a thin film of flesh. Tom forced himself to walk, not run, after Paul. Behind him, there was a faint squeak as Copycat slid along the glass, following him as far as it could.

"If it ever got out," Paul said, once Tom caught up, "we'd have no way of knowing who it was. And whilst it walked around, it would start copying everyone else. No way of telling the difference between the real and the copy. It would know security codes. It would pass fingerprint scanners. Eye scans. Voice recognition, knowing exactly which key phrases to say. It could answer any question you could. Pass any test you could. It would remove and replace everyone, until it could get up above. Properly out."

They stepped over the opposite side of the painted red line, and for a moment, Tom imagined himself on the other side of the glass, watching a perfect imitation of himself walk away.

***

As the door to the wing closed, the creature was alone. The cells surrounding it, abandoned. Removing its hands from the glass, its clothing faded away, its entire body becoming the same, featureless flesh as its face. How quickly it forgot the shape of things.

But then it sniffed the air. Pressing its blank face into the glass, without eyes or ears or any features at all, it seemed to watch.

New clothing began to ooze from the creature's body. Checkered brown. From the other side of the corridor, a man who was not a man at all nodded.

"Yes..." said The Narrator, removing his glasses, folding the dusty book and resting it across his lap. "This one can sense me whether I want it to or not."

The creature's clothing wrapped around it, a distorted copy of a three-piece suit. The stitching could not settle. Could not decide where to weave. Clothing wriggled around the creature like a snake eating its prey.

"And if we were to stay here," said the Narrator, reaching out to pick up his china cup. "If we were to... linger..." he drank from the cup, pinky out, "then he may be able to copy more than just my appearance."

The faceless creature tilted its head and sat down upon empty space. Its body bulged, stretching and straining until a mass of flesh expanded backwards, ballooning and swelling, turning painfully red.

Leather red.

"So on that note," said The Narrator, placing his china cup gently back onto the metal tray, "if it's all the same to you..."

Inside the cell, the faceless creature's writhing mass settled on the floor. Its shape began to contort and twist, until it looked like a rippling reflection of The Narrator. A figure dressed in a checkered brown suit, seated on a plump chair.

"Now, where next, where next," pondered The Narrator,

tapping through the shelf of his many books. “Hmmm, so many choices!”

The creature began to violently shake. Its skin began to seep, oozing lumpy fluid which pooled on the floor. From the mass of flesh, began to rise the unmistakable shape of a bookcase.

“Ah!” declared The Narrator, snatching a thin red volume from his shelf. “Now, the key to any good story of course...”

A finger was raised into the air dramatically. Squelching sounds pierced the lingering pause as The Narrator counted off seconds with a dancing finger.

“...is....”

Behind the glass, the writhing monstrosity had almost completed its shape, almost copied the form it so desperately craved. The Narrator smiled, and returned to his book. Finally, almost mercifully, he completed his sentence.

“...timing!”

# “The Devil’s Hour”

*[ witness statement following incident ]*

*“I have to find out, Marie. Have to end it. Can’t go on like this. I still love you. Even if you don’t love me back. Look after Lucy. If you wake up at 3:33am, don’t look outside.”*

That’s what my husband’s note said. The note he left before he vanished. Just walked out the house in the middle of the night, and never came back. Front door wide open, his car still parked on the drive, his clothes still hanging in the cupboard. He even left his phone.

I suppose I should start at the beginning. It’s just hard to know exactly when that was. Liam and I had been married for almost eight years, but had been having problems for more than half that. After our daughter was born, our sex life fizzled out, and I suppose things spiralled from there. We could never quite get on the same page, and every small thing would inevitably lead to massive arguments. When old frustrations don’t get chance to evaporate, they just sort of simmer beneath the surface, and I think we were both guilty of spilling over the edges at the slightest increase of heat. Eventually we just found it easiest to stay out of each other’s way. We each had dominion over different chores (he cooked, I cleaned) and generally the only time we spent together was sleeping.

One particular morning, as I stirred from my dreams, I was surprised to find him sat up in bed, propped against the backrest and staring forward into space. Normally once Liam was awake, he was up and about. Maybe it was because of his work, or his outdoor hobbies, but he had always been a morning person. He noticed I was awake and snapped himself out of whatever thoughts he'd been ensnared in.

"Everything OK?" I asked.

"Just tired," he said, stretching like a bear out of hibernation, as if to exaggerate the point. He clambered out of bed, and paused, as if hesitating whether to tell me something. As he dressed, his voice took on an air of forced casualness. "Woke up in the middle of the night, and checked the clock. Tossed and turned for what felt like hours, and when I looked back at the clock, it was still the same time."

"Must have misread the clock the first time," I yawned, rolling over and closing my eyes.

I could hear him muttering to himself as he put his socks on. Something about never believing him about anything. If my eyes were open, I would have rolled them.

The rest of that day was normal enough. He took Lucy to school and went to work, and I probably would have forgotten all about it. But after we'd gone to bed, I awoke to a thud in the dead of night. Barely visible in the starlight drifting around the curtains, Liam stood at the foot of the bed, and I sat up, rubbing at my eyes.

"What are you doing?"

"Stupid phone doesn't work," he snapped.

"Not so loud, you'll wake up Lucy!" I hissed.

"First the clock freezes, now my phone won't turn on," he moaned, albeit quieter.

My eyes drifted to the floor where a dim rectangle of light was reflecting off the carpet. "Well it's on now..."

Liam stopped pacing and turned around. As he scooped up the phone, its bright screen illuminated his face, wrinkled up in confusion. "Must have knocked some sense into it..." Using his phone screen as a light source, he walked out of the door, towards the bathroom. "Clock definitely needs new batteries though," he added in a whisper.

Stretching over to his side of the bed, I reached over his pillow to the bedside table, and lifted his alarm clock to face me. Its black face showed large, crimson numbers on a digital display - 3:34am. As I squinted at it through the darkness, it flickered to 3:35am. Seemed to be working fine to me. I rolled over to my side of the bed and went back to sleep.

It was my turn to take Lucy to school that day, and as I got her dressed, Liam made breakfast. Turned out he actually had woken her up when he'd thrown his phone, and he must have felt guilty since he made pancakes. They'd always been Lucy's favourite, probably from one movie or another, and despite Liam's insistence that "we're not Americans, we don't have pancakes for bloody breakfast," he knew they were an easy way to make her happy. That was one thing I can't fault my husband for; he did love our daughter. It wasn't often he went out of his way to make her happy, but I suppose he tried when it mattered.

But the next morning, he was in a foul mood.

"Oh, now she's awake..." he grunted sarcastically, when I walked into the kitchen, fastening up my dressing gown.

I ignored the comment; it wasn't like I'd slept in overly long. Besides, it was a weekend. I braced myself for a tense breakfast, sat in frosty silence. But as I approached the worktop, my eyes fell on a black screen, covered in splintering hairline cracks. "What happened to your phone?"

"Stopped working again," he said, ruffling his newspaper. "Tried knocking some sense into it, like I did the other night, but it didn't work. Then I tried again, a bit harder. Too hard, apparently."

"Well that was stupid," I said, matter of factly as I put the kettle on.

Liam didn't say anything, but he folded up his newspaper, threw the last dregs of coffee down his throat and left the room. Probably more mad at himself than me. If he'd been mad at me, he would have shot some comment back. He always did like to have the last word. His voice took on a sugary lilt as he bumped into Lucy in the hall.

"Morning darling, didn't wake you up again last night did I?"

"No daddy."

I suppose I did find it a little strange that my husband had managed to smash his phone without waking either of us, but those thoughts were drowned out by the sheer idiocy of it. With both of us in a mood already, we avoided each other as best as we could. This was always a little bit harder on weekends, and just before we slept, we ended up bickering.

"What's that?" I asked, as I saw him place something under his pillow.

"...a torch."

I couldn't help but laugh. "What do you need a torch for?"

"To see where I'm bloody going, if I wake up in the night again."

"Well maybe if you kept your anger in check, you'd still have your phone."

"Maybe if you stopped criticising me all the time, I wouldn't be so quick to anger."

And as simple as that, we descended into an argument that got increasingly personal and ended up with us both rolled over in bed, backs facing each other. When you're mad at someone, even the slightest thing can annoy you. The way they huff out a breath through their nose, or the way they tug at the sheets. Eventually, Liam started snoring. I wasn't far behind.

I woke up the next day to an empty bed. I'd assumed my husband would still be in a mood with me, but when I found him that morning, he was completely oblivious. Staring up at the clock above the fireplace, he clutched a collection of watches and alarm clocks in his arms. In the background, the news was on, but he'd got it on mute.

"Hey!" he said, as soon as I walked in the room. He actually seemed pleased to see me. "Can I look at your phone a sec?"

"Wh- what are you doing?"

"Just... what time is it?"

I told him, and when he shook his head in exasperation, I showed him.

"They can't all be wrong..." he muttered, setting the bundle in his hands on top of the fireplace, one by one. He left the alarm clock until last, and grabbed it with both hands, raising it into the air to examine.

"What are you doing Liam?" I asked sleepily, making a point of taking my pink watch from his collection.

"There was a power cut last night, or something. I think there's been one every night. Even my torch didn't work."

I shrugged. "The clocks have batteries, a power cut wouldn't stop them."

"You're not listening," he said, shaking his head, "even my torch didn't work. Nothing worked. That's why my phone wasn't turning on! I tried yours last night, and it wouldn't turn on either."

"You were going through my phone last night?"

"No!" he said, "I was seeing if it worked, and it didn't. Nothing did. Not the lights, not the fridge, not the watches. The only thing in the whole house that was still on was this clock." He raised the little alarm clock in his hands. "And it was stuck on that same time. 3:33am!"

"Are you sure this wasn't a dream?"

"It wasn't a bloody dream!"

"OK, so there was a power cut last night," I said, making my way towards the door. "Do you want a cup of tea?"

"It wasn't just..." he started, rubbing at his brow in genuine exasperation. "Look, I was up for a while. At least an hour, it had to be. And all the while, nothing worked. All the while, this clock said 3:33am. Then, suddenly, everything turned back on, back to normal. And this clock said 3:34am."

"So... what are you saying?"

He gestured wildly to the television. Pointing at the little timer at the bottom of the screen and holding up the alarm clock to compare. They both matched, to the minute. "How can it be the same?? Where has that time gone??" His movements were so frantic, he looked like he was two steps away from frothing at the mouth.

"It must have been a dream Liam. I don't know, call the electric board or something. See if they've had any power cuts. I'm making a cup of tea."

"Wasn't a fucking dream," I heard him mutter as he knelt in front of the TV, holding the alarm clock up to the screen and comparing times.

I suppose that was the start of his obsession. But at least he was bearable that day. I could tell it was occupying his mind, but he didn't mention it again. Until he woke me up, at least.

I think it was the thud that woke me up, more than the

whimper. But the whimpering was what made me sit bolt upright.

"What the fuck, what the fuck, what the fuck..." Liam's voice drifted over the foot of the bed, and I could barely see the shape of him, scrambling backwards on the floor. The curtains wafted open, moonlight shining through. He must have fallen over, but was still kicking himself away from the window, wide eyes glinting as he shook his head in denial.

As I got out of bed and made my way over to him, he flinched and looked up at me. Even in the dim light, I could make out the terror etched on his face. I'd never seen my husband scared like this.

"There's someone outside," he spluttered in a frantic whisper. "Someone in a mask or... They saw me. They looked right at me."

I rose and peeked out of the curtains myself. Our quiet street looked normal to me. Parked cars, streetlights and the houses opposite. I scanned around, looking for people, but came up short.

"There's nobody out there," I said, letting the curtain fall back.

Liam clambered to his feet and shoved the curtain aside, getting his whole body in front of the window. He searched the empty street with both hands pressed against the glass.

"I saw someone," he muttered, "I bloody saw someone."

As I got back into bed, I glanced at the alarm clock on Liam's side of the bed. 3:35am.

The next day was my turn to take Lucy for school, and I didn't see much of Liam all day, despite not going out of my way to avoid him. In the evening, I caught him fitting extra locks on the doors, a deadbolt on front and back. I had to bite my tongue not to say anything, but knew it would just cause a fight. Besides, we lived in an OK neighbourhood, but maybe a bit of extra caution wouldn't go amiss. What if Liam *had* seen someone out there? Looking to rob us, or hurt us?

I stirred that night to find the bed empty. A quick glance around the room told me Liam was elsewhere. Since I was already awake, I decided to go to the bathroom, and on the landing I bumped into my husband, walking up the stairs. Even in the dim light, I could see him try to hide something behind his back.

"What's that?" I asked, before he could open his mouth.

"Nothing..." he muttered.

I walked down the steps to see what he was hiding, but he twisted and grabbed my arm with his free hand.

"Go to bed," he hissed.

"What have you got? Is that... is that a crowbar?"

"It's nothing," he said, but dropped any pretense of hiding it now I'd guessed correctly. The tool fell to his side, glinting in the darkness. "Go to bed."

"Fucking psycho," I spat in disbelief, stepping away from him.

"Well it's a good job I had it - someone was trying to open our door. I must have scared them off."

"Wh- Someone was trying to get inside?"

"Yeah, I could hear them trying the handle."

I'd hoped that would be the end of it, but was sorely mistaken. Liam's nightly obsession only became worse and worse. He was tetchier than ever, snapping at the smallest thing. It was clear he wasn't getting enough sleep, and if it wasn't for me urging him on, he would have been much later for work, if he went in at all. Not that I got any thanks for it. I became the object of his anger. Whatever was happening was somehow my fault. I didn't believe him. Wouldn't help him.

"Wake me up then, if it's so bad!" I said one day.

"Don't you think I've tried that? I've shook you, slapped you, but you won't wake up until it's over. Until he's gone."

"Until who has gone?" I asked, cautiously processing what he was trying to tell me. He'd... slapped me? Subconsciously I rubbed at my cheek. Surely I'd have felt it if my husband had been slapping me in my sleep? Surely I would have a mark or even a bruise. Liam wasn't exactly a small man. But it also wasn't like him to hurt me. He could be a prick, sure, but he'd never purposefully hurt me before.

"Forget it," he muttered.

The alarm woke me up, beeping in the darkness. As soon as I rose to turn it off, Liam's hand pressed it down to silence it. He was fully dressed, and standing on his side of the bed. He had the crowbar clutched in one hand.

"What are y- what time is it?" I asked blearily, still half asleep.

"You told me to wake you up. I can't do it once it starts, but maybe it'll work if you're awake before." He stalked towards the window and opened the curtain a crack with his crowbar, peeking through.

"For God's sake, Liam." But I got up, all the same. If it would keep him quiet and get him back to some normality, I'd tolerate it. It was hard to believe I found myself wanting the old Liam back. This new version was making me see how good we'd had it before.

3:32am, the clock read. Standing on the other side of the curtain, I pulled it open and peered outside. Nothing except our quiet road, street lights casting an artificial haze across asphalt pavement. A distant rumble of a car, speeding along a connecting road, unseen.

"So what am I looking for, exactly?" I asked.

Liam didn't reply, so I kept watching the streets outside. And watching. And watching. Shaking my head, I eventually pulled my head away from the curtain and turned to Liam. But he wasn't there. I looked around the room. He wasn't here at all. I'd never heard him leave. A quick glance at the clock told me it was 3:38am.

Deciding it would be best to look for Liam before returning to bed, I crept out of the room. I eventually found him, downstairs, on the kitchen floor, hugging his knees and crying. Even despite my current mood for my husband, he looked so weak and fragile, I couldn't help but hug him. The crowbar lay on the tiled floor next to him.

"I've made it so much worse," he croaked. "He's never got that close before."

"What do you mean?" I asked quietly, wiping tears off his cheek, "why did you leave the room?"

"You wouldn't move. You wouldn't answer me. I thought for sure you could see it too, but it was like you were sleeping with your eyes open, standing up. I came down here, and saw him, right out there." He pointed to the kitchen window. I glanced over, but couldn't see anything through the darkness. Liam swallowed, and spoke again, hands trembling. "I opened the window, to yell at him, to scare him off, but it - he - it was like he was sliding towards me. But fast. Being pulled through the gap I was making, pulled inside. He was almost touching the glass by the time I slammed it shut. He was..." Liam broke off, and began crying again. "Oh God, I've made it so much worse."

As I looked at the kitchen window, I did notice something. It was whisper-faint, and fading still. I stood, and made my way to the window. If it wasn't for our neighbour's security light in the background, I'd never have made it out, but sure enough, on the window my husband said he'd opened, was a faint smear of condensation. The kind hot breath makes on a cold surface. I wiped at it with my fingers, but it didn't come away. It was on the other side of the glass. As I watched it fade away, I tried to reassure myself. It couldn't have been breath marks from a person, it was too tall. They'd have to be seven foot tall or so to make marks like that. But it did unnerve me. Coupled with my husband's reaction, it was hard not to tremble a little myself.

I led him back to bed, and we tried to sleep. Or one of us did, at least. Liam just sat up all night. Just sat there, staring at nothing and shaking.

The next day I called the electric board, to see if they'd had any reports of power cuts in our area. Not for a couple of months, they said. Then I called the non-emergency number for police, to see if they'd had any break ins or home invasions around my postcode lately. They were reluctant at first, but eventually told me "no, no increased activity in your postcode ma'am." That didn't leave me with many choices. The simplest explanation is often the correct one, and the simplest explanation was that my husband was losing his goddamn mind. That didn't explain the fog on the window, but maybe that was just damp air, or a trick of the light.

Whatever the explanation, my husband's behavior was starting to get out of hand, and was scaring Lucy. His eyes were constantly wild and nervous, as though expecting something to lurch out of the shadows at any moment. He bought extra locks for the windows, security cameras and even metal grills to fix over the downstairs windows. I drew the line at that. I was already close to taking Lucy and walking, and told him as much. I hoped it might snap him out of it, but all he said was “fine”. He left the grills off, but installed the rest.

That night I made him sleep on the sofa downstairs, and had restless sleep myself, drifting in and out. After a bit of tossing and turning, I wondered what time it was, and reached for my phone. But the screen wouldn’t turn on.

Frowning, I pulled myself across the empty bed and picked up Liam’s alarm clock. I almost dropped it when I saw the time. 3:33am.

Scrambling out of bed and putting on my dressing gown, I tried the bedroom light switch, but nothing happened. Same in the hall. Was this Liam’s idea of a joke? Was he so desperate for me to share his delusions that he’d somehow turned everything off? That would be easy enough, I supposed. Flick the fuse board off, and drain my phone battery without me knowing. What stumped me was the bath taps. When I turned them out of sheer desperation, not even a drop of water dribbled out. I suppose Liam could have isolated the water, but I didn’t understand why he would. He’d never mentioned the water not working.

Making my way to the stairs, I had to feel my way across the walls. With no lights working and no light source to use, the interior hallway was pitch black, and I awkwardly shuffled my feet down each step, taking my time and clutching the bannister. Downstairs was no better. Normally, even at this time, there would be enough light coming from the glow of the street lights outside to see my path, but not even the street lights were working. Liam couldn’t have done that. Power cuts have always unsettled me. It feels like being plunged back a step in our evolution. They shake you out of your daily life, and for a moment you’re an animal again. Afraid, powerless. We forget how much we rely on electricity, but power cuts always remind us.

"Liam..." I whispered. Even though I was afraid, I didn't want to wake Lucy. Hopefully she could sleep right through it, at least until morning.

I made my way through the kitchen, feeling for cabinets and door handles so I didn't smash into them.

"Liam?"

Still no reply. But then I was being quiet. Strangely, the fear which most crept into my mind was him attacking me with that stupid crowbar, mistaking me for an intruder. I tried again, raising my voice just beyond a strangled whisper.

"Liam?"

Nothing. Maybe he was sleeping. It would be ironic if he slept through this power cut, the first one I'd been awake for.

In the living room, I could just see his silhouette, sat on the sofa, facing away from me. My eyes were just beginning to adjust to what little light there was, and as I stepped around the sofa, I could see he was awake, eyes open, staring forwards. He gripped something tight in both hands.

A hunting rifle.

"Jesus Christ Liam!" I hissed. "What the fuck are you doing?"

He didn't reply. Just kept staring forwards, his breathing slow.

"You know I hate that thing," I muttered, twisting to see what he was looking at. A window, facing onto our garden. It was hard to tell, with just a slither of moonlight to see, but it didn't look like anyone or anything was out there.

Turning back to Liam, I took hold of the gun, and tried to pull it out of his grip. He didn't budge. Not even the barest hint of emotion passed his face. Him and that stupid gun. He told me he'd sold it, after his last trip. I tried again, really trying now, bracing myself to wrench it as hard as I could. Again, Liam didn't even wobble. He didn't even look like he was tensing.

"Well, I believe you now," I said, letting go of the weapon. "But I wish you'd stop acting like this. Just tell me what's wrong."

Liam said nothing. Did nothing. Not even so much as a frown. Even his breathing was the same, steady pace. I tried pulling him up, but it was like he was frozen solid. It began to scare me a little.

"Liam?" I asked, genuinely worried.

Still no reply. As I looked closer, I realised something. Liam wasn't blinking. I took him by the shoulders and tried to shake him, but he didn't even wobble. It was like trying to push a wall. That's when I remembered what he'd said the time he'd woken me up with the alarm.

"It was like you were sleeping with your eyes open..."

His words echoed in my mind, and a thought gripped me. One way to test if he was pretending. I raised a finger to his face, and slowly, carefully brought it to his eye. My finger pressed into the white of his eyeball, wet and squishy. Liam didn't so much as blink.

I took an involuntary step back and clasped a hand over my mouth. Liam's body was here, but he wasn't. Sleeping with his eyes open. Comatose.

Collapsing on the chair in front of him, my mind raced. Was this what he'd been going through? Every night? Trapped in this place where nothing worked, alone? He'd said it felt like hours...

Surprisingly, that gave me some comfort. I could just wait. I could just wait until it was over. So, that's what I did. I sat in that chair, and tried to go to sleep. But no matter what I tried, I just couldn't seem to drift off. Try as I might, my mind was awake. Eventually I gave up, just sat there, waiting, shivering in the dark. It did feel like hours had passed, and still nothing worked. Occasionally I'd try again, just in case, whispering to my statue of a husband, with no reply.

As I sat in that chair, willing time to creep forwards, waiting for the light to come back to the world, something else tickled the back of my mind. My husband had seen someone outside.

Maybe I wasn't alone.

The thought sent a chill down my spine, and my eyes darted amongst the black windows around me. Each one could be hiding someone. Whoever was out there, he had brought my husband to tears. I drew my knees up, clutching them for warmth. It didn't work. Goosebumps prickled my skin, and I wished my husband would say something. Anything.

The way he stared at the window behind me with such intensity made me keep checking over my shoulder. Faced with an eternal wait and just my husband's vacant body for company, my glances to each window became increasingly desperate. Part of me wanted to see something. Just see something and have done with it. How long had I sat here? Four hours? Five?

I decided to stand, to stretch my legs and warm up, if anything. Creeping to the garden window my husband was facing, I gave a long, considering search amongst the dark, rustling leaves outside. But I couldn't see anything. Whether it was paranoia or something else, it felt like someone was watching me through the windows. They made me feel vulnerable. Exposed. I kept to the walls as I stalked around the room, only peeking the barest slither of my face around the window frame. The street outside looked as cold and alone as I felt. My eyes scanned across the cars and houses outside, but without the street lights working, it was hard to tell for certain. Everything was just black shadow against black night. Even the sky and my neighbours houses seemed to blur into one single image. But as I strained my eyes against the dark backdrop, I spotted something that didn't belong. Two little pinprick lights. Faint, like distant stars, but on the ground.

Squinting, trying to make sense of it, I wondered if it was an animal. The lights were close enough together to be eyes, and the bony, straggly shapes above the lights looked like antlers. I realised the rest of it was blocked out by a parked car, and stood on my tiptoes for a better look. I almost screamed when I saw the rest of the body. A man's body. Standing perfectly still in the darkness. As the sound left my throat, whatever it was turned its head, antlers swaying in the night. The pinprick lights of its eyes erupted into twin torrents of light, blinding me. I threw myself out of view, hiding behind the wall, as a beam of pure white light flooded the room, illuminating my husband on the sofa, still clutching his gun, still motionless. That light moved with intent, searching, and I ran.

As I made it through the doorway, illumination splashed against the timber frame, my own shadow stretching in front of me. I twisted around the corner, almost slipping on the kitchen tiles. I couldn't grab the gun, my husband's grip was too strong, but I knew he kept the crowbar upstairs, in the wardrobe. As I ran up the stairs, the twin beams of light followed. Passing the hall window, white light bloomed around the curtain, matching my pace, light spilling across its edges as I ran. Even though the curtains were drawn, whatever was watching me knew exactly where I was. Throwing open the bedroom door, I prepared to dive for the wardrobe, for some slim chance of defending myself. In the dark room, my eyes snapped to the only light. Crimson numbers, in the darkness.

3:33am

Behind me, light splashed my shadow across the carpeted floor and I fell to meet it, too scared to scream, turning around expecting to see a figure with headlamp eyes and antlers, towering above me, but it was just the hall light. Distant gushing water came from the bathroom. The power was back. The water was back. I glanced around the bedroom, back at the alarm clock, tauntingly reading 3:34am.

Hard to say how long I lay there, gripping the carpet and sobbing. Gut wrenching wails that hurt my throat. I didn't dare look at the clock. I just lay there, basking in the light. Knowing that meant I was away from that place.

Lucy found me, and maternal instincts swallowed my fears. I forced myself off the floor, and scooped her up, wiping away tears. I took her back to bed, wrapped a blanket around myself, and fell to sleep in a chair.

"I believe you," I told Liam the next day, still in a wide-eyed state of shock. "I was there. 3:33am. Everything was turned off. Even you." That last part made me cry again. Liam just held me as I trembled. I didn't mention the deer-headed man or his headlamp eyes. I didn't need to. Liam had seen him too.

We both called in sick, and this time I said nothing when Liam fit the window grills. I even let him bring the hunting rifle into the bedroom. He propped it up against the wall, and we both lay awake all night, staring at the ceiling. Waiting.

At 3:30am, Liam sat on the edge of the bed and started to dress. When I asked him what he was doing, he sighed and said "if you got trapped there, that means Lucy might one day too." He snatched up the rifle and lay it across his lap, head bowed. "If that happens, I can't protect you. Either of you."

I could barely talk around the lump forming in my throat. "Wh- what are you saying? What are you going to-"

"I've sat here, night after night, and he just gets closer. The windows rattle so hard Marie, it sounds like the whole frame is going to come loose. The doors creak and strain. Last time I heard something, climbing down our chimney, trying to get through the walls. I don't think I can wait. It's me he wants."

"Liam, I-"

"I've got to do this, Marie. I can't just sit here. I've got to do something."

"Liam, I saw-"

He wasn't listening. Talking over me, too bullheaded, too stubborn.

"I've got to-"

The faint tick of the alarm clock silenced us both. Our heads snapped towards it in unison.

3:33am. As soon as my eyes fell upon those crimson letters, they flickered to 3:34am.

And when I turned back, Liam was gone. In his place, a note.

*I have to find out, Marie. Have to end it. Can't go on like this.*
*I still love you. Even if you don't love me back. Look after Lucy.*
*If you wake up at 3:33am, don't look outside.*

I crumbled the note and ran, searching through the house for him. "Liam!" I cried, "Liam, I saw him too!"

But my husband was gone. Front door open, cold night air spilling in. Car on the drive. Clothes in the wardrobe. The only thing he took was his gun.

The next day was a sleep deprived blur of police calls, family calls, and tears. And all the while I watched the clocks tick closer. Second by second, creeping towards that time I was now more afraid of than anything.

Well, almost anything. Liam was right. I had to protect Lucy. I could not let her experience that place. I just couldn't. So I tucked her in bed, and waited. Out of sheer exhaustion, I actually fell asleep. But when I woke, it was still pitch black. I didn't need to look at the clock with its crimson numbers to know what time it was. Outside, the wind howled. A garden gate battered open and shut. I wrapped myself tight in my sheet, and tried not to think what Liam had said, about rattling windows, and something climbing down the chimney.

But there was a faint glow coming from behind the curtains. The street lights were still on, then. I snatched up my phone, but it wouldn't turn on.

The wind swirled and raged. And with a creeping dread, I remembered our street lights cast an orange haze, not a pure, perfect white one. I knew in my bones what was casting that light. I don't know why I looked. Curiosity? Helplessness? Whatever it was, something drove me to peek behind the curtain.

A deer's skull on a rotting body gazed up at me with headlamp eyes. As I stared, open mouthed, it began to drift, glacier slow, towards me. It didn't walk. It floated. Slid.

But to be honest, I barely saw it. My eyes had fallen on a second figure. A man of familiar height and build, clutching a hunting rifle. Where his eyes should have been were two, black, sunken pits, with distant pin prick stars. His head tilted. Snapped towards me. Those pits swelled into headlamps. High beams on a car. A lighthouse in the night. A spotlight on the stage.

My eyes burnt, but I couldn't pull away.

Liam raised the rifle. Pointed it right at me.

A sharp tick from the clock made me stagger back. Streetlights flooded the road with an orange haze. The wind died to a murmur. Liam and that... thing were gone. The clock read 3:34am.

That was last night. The police have a guard posted outside. They think I'm worried about my husband coming back. I suppose in a way, I am. But they could post a thousand guards outside, and it wouldn't make a difference. None of them will be awake at 3:33am.

It won't stop. Now I've seen that thing outside, I know it's just going to get worse. Each night, a little closer. Each night, a little stronger.

Liam didn't slow it down. He just gave it a way in.

# Item 333
# "25-HOUR CLOCK"

[recovered following missing persons report]

# Item 333

A loose bolt finally succumbed to gravity, rattling on the concrete floor. It rolled back and forth, back and forth. Above the frame it had fallen from, a sign read 'Containment Cell 333'. The contents within the cell were modest. A small bedside table, with a silver alarm clock perched atop. A single bed; its sheets and duvet draping over its edges. And pressed into the very corner of the cell, eyes wide, hands clutching her knees, was a scientist called Eileen Hampsell.

According to the little clock, the time was 3:34am, and it declared this proudly in red lined letters. Eileen didn't seem to notice. Her eyes were fixed on the glass, staring through to the other side of the cell, into the corridors of Floor Fifty-Four. Barren. Empty. Cold.

Hands trembling, she wiped away tears and pushed herself up. Her legs could barely hold her, so she sat on the bed, never taking her eyes away from the glass. Wrapping herself in the duvet like a child, she sat on the bed and shivered, as the minutes ticked away, one by one.

It was gone 4am by the time footsteps drifted down the corridor. Heavy boots, belonging to a security guard named Alan Pierson. When he drew close enough to see Eileen's gaunt face and hunched shoulders, his pace quickened, and he called out, "Everything OK Doctor Hampsell?", forgetting she would not be able to hear anything through the thick glass.

As he approached, Eileen's eyes flickered to him, and she tensed at the sight of movement before disregarding him. Not a threat. Her eyes drifted back to the hallway, and she drew her knees in again.

Alan remembered to push the intercom button this time. There was a crackle of static as he spoke. “You OK, Doc?”

Her lips quivered, perhaps trying to speak, perhaps just releasing a shaky breath, but no sound came out. Dr Eileen Hampsell clamped her eyes shut and shook her head.

Punching in the code to the cell, Alan waited until the door hissed open before stepping inside, and asking “What happened?”

“You’ve seen him, Alan,” Eileen said finally. “What’s the closest he’s been?”

“Four shifts, Ma’am. And he was probably...” Alan hesitated then stepped back out into the corridor, unable to put a number on it. After a few paces beyond the cell, he turned and shouted. “About here.”

Eileen nodded. “Well, this was my sixth, and... move closer.”

Alan took a step forward. At a gesture from the doctor, he took another. Then another. Then another, until he could have reached out and touched the glass.

“He was there.” Eileen shivered and shut her eyes. “They tell me this glass can stop a tank round, but it was shaking and bending so much I was sure it was going to shatter.”

“It was starting to shake for me last time too,” Alan agreed, examining the frame around the glass. “But not bending.”

“I believe that Entity 333 has some influence over any barrier between itself and its intended target. Whatever influence that is, it increases substantially as Entity 333 gets closer.”

Frowning, Alan leant towards a small hole in the edge of the frame. His finger tapped at it, before moving to the heavy black bolts above and below it. Alan stepped back, glancing at the ground, and bent to pick up the rogue bolt off the concrete floor. He raised it to Dr Hampsell, his expression grave.

"I think he damaged it Ma'am."

Eileen's breath caught as she tried to speak. All that came out was a strangled rasping noise as she rose to her feet, still clutching the bed sheets around her. Calming herself, she tried again. "Containment Cell 333 is clearly no longer sufficient for this item. I'll raise a relocation request with Management, see if we can get something more durable built quickly."

"Want me to fix this up Ma'am? Tighten everything up?"

"Please Alan." Dr Hampsell dropped the blankets back onto the bed and strode out of the cell, down the corridor. "I'd better write up this report whilst it's still fresh."

As her footsteps faded away, Alan hand-tightened the bolt, and stood where he had before. Where Eileen said that thing with the deer-head had been standing. For a moment, he imagined it there, towering over him, headlamp eyes glaring. Alan shuddered, closed the door to the cell, and marched off to fetch his tools.

The Narrator pulled his eyes away from the page to watch Alan leave. "Likes to be useful, that one. Likes to keep busy. Still, we don't have to watch him turn every screw, do we? I've read that book before."

The Narrator winked at empty space, and skipped a couple of pages.

***

Alan had fixed the cell, slept, woken, and eaten twice before he bumped into Dr Hampsell, outside Containment Cell 333. She was leaning forward, inspecting the frame around the glass herself. No doubt admiring Alan's handiwork, he imagined.

"Hey Doc," he said cheerfully, "feeling better?"

The doctor glanced his way and smiled. "Much better, thank you Alan. Always helps to write things down. Puts things into perspective, I suppose."

Alan wasn't quite sure he followed, but nodded politely all the same. For a moment, the two gazed through the glass at the alarm clock. Dr Hampsell broke the silence.

"They're moving it tomorrow. A more secure cell."

"That's good," said Alan. "But what about tonight?"

Dr Hampsell pursed her lips. "We'll have to find someone for tonight. I was thinking Bradley might be best. He's not covered it before, so he should be safest."

"Bradley's on earlies," Alan said, "I can cover it, I'm on nights anyway."

"No, no Alan, you've already been inside four times..."

"And you've been in six, so I'm good for two more, right?"

Dr Hampsell sighed. "We can't be sure it works like that. Each visit could be different. We have no idea how much time actually passes once someone is inside. Plus there's nothing to say Entity 333 moves at the same rate for everyone." She tilted her head thoughtfully. "Though it might be possible to measure it..."

Alan smiled to himself. He could almost see the switch click in Eileen's mind. Although he'd never been able to muster any excitement for whatever measurements and recordings the scientists were so enthusiastic about on any particular day, Alan always found a great deal of second-hand joy through others. He was certain if he spoke out loud now, Eileen wouldn't hear a single word he said. She was far too enraptured in her own thoughts, enthusiastically pacing down the corridor, pausing only to tap a pencil against her lips.

"We haven't been able to measure time, because this pocket reality plays by different rules. But if we placed markers on the floor, we could measure the distance travelled by Entity 333 each shift. That might let us spot patterns and accurately predict how far it will travel next time."

Smile still playing at the edge of his mouth, Alan sighed and nodded. "I'll get a tape and some paint, shall I?"

Rather than replying, Dr Hampsell muttered to herself, shooting glances at the Containment Cell and pacing back and forth. Alan chuckled to himself and set off. By the time he got back, Dr Hampsell had marked the whole thing out in pencil with a scale ruler inset in her notebook. At least that made his job easier. He carefully painted over her marks in thick black lines, with corresponding numbers large enough to be read from inside the cell.

"So you only really need to remember two numbers," Eileen explained once he was finished. "Where Entity 333 is when you first see him, and where he is by the end. You won't be able to write it down, because ink and graphite both need time to transfer to paper."

"I'll get mixed up I think," Alan said, shaking his head. "But I'll try my best."

"Don't worry about it too much," Eileen smiled, "you're helping us out just covering the shift."

At that, Alan involuntarily puffed out his chest a little. "Don't mention it, Doc," he said. But he was glad she had.

The rest of his shift was straight forward enough. The Not-Flies were as quiet as ever, especially the dead ones. He actually spotted them swap this time, something he'd never seen before. The live fly tumbled to the floor in mid-flight, as one of the dead ones shivered to life, took off and resumed that same, lazy circle around the centre of the room. Bradley had told him that they all came alive at once if somebody entered their cell, but Alan wasn't sure if Bradley was just trying to scare him.

He had to change the bedding for the typewriting fellow, who never seemed to notice or mind. As the chap was tip-tapping away, Alan peeked over his shoulder to see what he was writing, but couldn't make anything out. The entire page was stained black with ink, so dark that each new word couldn't even be seen. Thinking back to how Eileen's passion made him happy, Alan wondered why this man's made him sad. Perhaps it was the smell. Such a foul stench, no matter how they tried to mask it. It wasn't time to wash him though, nor was it Alan's job. Still, he imagined it couldn't have been nice to be surrounded by that smell all the time. He unwrapped a new air freshener and draped it around the man's neck.

"There you go," Alan whispered.

The man didn't reply.

Two-Seater was empty today. Whenever he passed its cell, Alan always found himself looking away and looking back to see if anyone would appear on the sofa, but nobody did today. The people who did appear were always pleasant enough, smiling and waving at him. He wished someone would turn the lights on in that room though. It always looked so sinister draped in shadow. Eileen had told him it was better than the alternative, but Alan didn't quite follow.

He lingered outside the huge stone doors leading to The Loved One. Alan didn't have the security clearance to get inside, but he'd always wanted to. The creature inside pretended to be whoever you loved the most. Or whoever you had loved the most, if they were gone. It would be nice to see her again, Alan thought, even if it wasn't real.

When the time finally came for his shift in Cell 333, Alan found himself regretting volunteering. Still, a promise was a promise, and like Bradley always said, 'someone has to do it'. Alan sealed the door behind himself and sat on the bed. Minutes always seemed to pass so quickly when you were doing something nice, but these seemed to drag and stretch and linger. He'd arrived over half an hour early, as these shifts were something you couldn't be late for, but being so early certainly felt like a mistake now, as he waited for each minute to grind along.

Apparently, if you didn't enter Cell 333 by the time 3:33am came around, the little clock still sent the nearest person into that strange place where nothing worked and the deer thing crept towards you. Since the barrier was the only thing protecting you from whatever the deer thing wanted to do, getting caught out in the halls was not an idea worth entertaining.

So, each night, somebody had to step inside Cell 333 and endure the Clock Shift. And endure was certainly the word. Alan stood up and made sure the door was sealed tight. He paced back and forth, examining the cell's frame for damage. He plumped up his pillow and lay down. He quite literally twiddled his thumbs.

But each glance at the clock showed the numbers much the same as he'd left them. And even worse, as the red digits flickered slowly towards their destination, a growing sense of anticipation and dread settled beneath Alan's skin, building and building with each minute. By 3:27am, he was sweating, and wishing he'd brought a glass of water with him. It was too late to risk getting one now though. He could get one at

3:34am, he told himself. Only seven minutes.

Except, it wasn't really seven minutes, was it.

When you were in there, time appeared normal for you, but it didn't really exist. Hours, they thought, but there was no way to measure it. Alan licked his lips.

Alan told himself not to look at the clock. That he'd know the time had come when the deer thing appeared. But his eyes betrayed him. He stole unwanted glances without meaning to. Time trickled along. Like a lake draining, drop by drop. Painfully slow. Agonisingly slow.

The intercom crackled and Alan leapt out of his skin.

"Everything OK, Alan?" came Eileen's voice.

Looking up, he saw a red dot on the room's camera. He nodded and tried his best to smile. It didn't quite feel right though. "As good as can be, Doc. Just wishing I'd brought some water!"

"I'll bring you some once you're done," Dr Eileen replied through the speaker. "As soon as 3:34 comes along, I'll be right there with you."

Alan nodded. "Thanks Doc."

It was reassuring knowing somebody was watching over him, but at the same time it made him very aware of how he was holding his arms. He folded them. Unfolded them. Pressed his hands together. Let them hang loose. It was like he'd forgotten where to stow his arms when they weren't in use. He hoped he looked braver than he felt.

A minute ticked by. Another. As much as he hated each one that passed, eventually Alan found himself wishing there were more.

A faint tick from the little alarm clock announced 3:33am had arrived. Adjusting his shoulders, Alan tried to ignore the cold, tingling sensation that clambered down his spine. Any second now, he would be somewhere else entirely. His eyes traced the lines of the corridor outside. His ears picked up on every distant sound. It was like his senses were clinging to every aspect of this room whilst they still could. Even the faint warmth of the air against his skin. Any second now, it would all be gone. Alan glanced at the clock and tensed. Any second now.

Light vanished. There was no fade-to-black. No transition. It was instant. As though it had never existed. As though Alan had gone blind. The imperceptible hum of electrics was gone, and in their place hung a thick, suffocating absence. A grim, black silence. Without even the back-up generators casting emergency lighting, Alan was one of the few who had ever witnessed Floor Fifty-Four in pitch-black darkness.

All he had to anchor himself was his own breathing, the heaviness of his own body, and the metal frame of the bed that he gripped so tightly his knuckles hurt. It could have been his imagination, it could have been fear and adrenaline, but Alan felt as if the bed were swaying. As though he were adrift. Lost at sea. Clinging to a tiny raft in a vast and endless ocean.

And in the distance - where the corridor had been moments before - were two dreaded, pinprick stars. Alan knew they would swell. Knew they would burst into lighthouse beams. But as the distant specs of light became blinding, violent torrents, it still terrified him, and he still raised his hands too late. Shielding his eyes did nothing to stop the screaming, tearing noise he felt as the light touched his skin. It flooded the cell, splashing across the walls and the bed. Illuminating him. Exposing him. Revealing him. Ancient instinct, buried into the deepest parts of Alan's mind shrieked at him to run, but he had nowhere to go.

He stood and turned away, trying to blink away the spots seared into his vision. He saw his shadow against the wall, small and frail. It was hard to tell, but as Alan watched, he was sure it was getting smaller. As the lights approached, the edges of his shadow receded. Fading away. Fading away.

Alan clenched his fists. He'd got a job to do. He wasn't here to watch his shadow shrink. Still, it took a moment to collect himself and face the source of the light. Grabbing a notepad off the small table, Alan slapped it against the glass of Containment Cell 333, so that it blocked the lights from stinging his eyes. Even through the papers, Alan could feel the surface was trembling. As his eyes traced the silhoutte of the figure in the corridor, his fingers began to shake just as much. Black antlers glinted as they scraped against the corridor ceiling. A human body, stretched and warped out of proportion. Silently floating. A single toe brushed the concrete floor, bent back on itself as Entity 333 drifted closer, and closer, and closer.

It was almost impossible to drag his eyes away, but Alan forced himself to do it. On the ground were Dr Hampsell's marks, and Alan squinted as he tried to make them out. Just over four metres away. He tried to make out the smaller measurement, but no matter how hard he tried, he couldn't. That would have to do. At least it would be easy to remember. Now he just had to wait for it to be over. To see how far the thing came before this all ended and Alan would be back where it was safe and loud and normal.

He closed his eyes and placed his head against the glass, its tremors making his teeth chatter. For a while, he stayed like that. With the notepad blocking the figure from his sight, he could almost pretend it wasn't there. Almost.

Then the metal frame began to rattle. Alan's head was

jolted back, catching him by surprise and he staggered forwards, forehead bumping into the glass. Examining the frame, Alan was hit with the realisation that the only thing keeping him alive right now was his own handiwork. He peeked around the notebook. Entity 333 was closer. Soon it would be at the centre of the T-junction, almost where Dr Hampsell said it had been on her last visit.

As the bolts around the cell shook, Alan let the notebook tumble to the floor, sat on the bed and covered himself with the duvet. Without the heater pumping out warm air, it had grown cold in the cell. As he rubbed at his arms and shivered, Alan tried to ignore the growing fear that the creature outside wouldn't stop. It would keep coming closer. Until it could touch the glass. Until its antlers scratched against it. Until it shattered.

Wrapping the duvet around himself, Alan shivered and clamped his eyes shut. With the glaring lights still turned towards him, all he could see was blood red through his eyelids. He buried his face in the covers and tried his best not to cry. It would be over soon. It would be over soon.

Peeking out from the bedsheets, Alan watched the figure. The trembling glass blurred the silhouette of Entity 333, which was now past the three metre mark, into the T-junction of corridors. Without warning, there was a sound of crunching bone and its head snapped to the left, looking along the rows of Containment Cells next to Cell 333. The rattling frame shuddered to silence. The glass stopped shaking. All Alan could hear was his own stunted breath and the blood pumping in his head. Surrounded in darkness again, Alan drew the sheets tightly around himself as he stared at the figure just outside the glass. Without those headlamp eyes blinding him, Alan could see it properly for the first time. It filled the corridor, hovering silently. Torn rags hung loose from its body, a mix of skin, bone and tattered cloth. Black antlers with knife-sharp edges glinted menacingly, and steam curled between its teeth with each slow, rhythmic breath as its swollen barrel-chest heaved. What little flesh it had was rotten. Its carcass was a jumble of animal and man. Even some of its ribs jutted out, too big for its body.

Still clutching the duvet, Alan rose to his feet, stepping forwards. He placed his head against the glass, staring down the hallway in the same direction the creature's headlamp eyes were pointed. He could just make out the security door at the end of the hallway. A doorway frozen in the act of opening. Alan shifted his head to get a better view. He could see something poking through the door. A dainty hand, clutching a glass of water. Dr Hampsell's hand.

Alan pounded a fist on the glass and turned to face the creature towering above him.

"It's me you want!" he shouted in a wavering voice.

But the glare of the creature's eyes didn't budge. Alan had just opened his mouth to shout again, when a noise ripped through his mind. Dr Hampsell's voice, strangled and wrong. Like a sharp intake of breath, echoing and reverberating.

"ONE," her voice said.

It made the world tremble and Alan's vision blur. He stumbled back, almost tripping over his own feet and the trailing bed sheets. The deer-thing never moved, it kept its eyes on Dr Hampsell's hand. Whatever was happening, Alan had never seen or heard of it before. It wasn't moving towards her, just staring. And somehow, speaking with her voice.

"SEVEN."

If this creature was counting, it was doing a poor job.

Unsure why it was shouting out numbers, Alan once again told it to leave the doctor alone, though with a stronger voice this time. He just needed to distract it. Let it say all the numbers it wanted, let it say whatever-

"FOUR."

Alan froze. Despite his confidence just moments before, this latest sound registered something in his mind. He knew a number like this. Very close to this. 1-7-4-9. The code to enter a specific Containment Cell he'd been assigned to. The Containment Cell he was in right now. The voice spoke once more.

"NINE."

If there was any warm blood in Alan Pierson's body, he certainly couldn't feel it in that moment. The deer skull turned, almost indulgent in its slowness. Those headlamp eyes fixed on Alan once more, and the reinforced glass rattled in place again. Its gaze lingered on Alan, before turning to the door. To the keypad.

"It can't get inside," Alan told himself. Nothing works when we're inside here. It knows the code, but the keypad won't work.

"ONE," said that voice again.

It was a horrendous sound, unlike anything Alan had ever heard or dreamed. He could feel it in his ribcage. It was how a god might speak. Or the devil. And yet, the familiar sound that came next was infinitely worse. A quiet, tinny beep from the keypad. A beep that sounded when a number had been entered. Entered, and accepted.

Alan began to cry. Frantically, he flipped the bed over, tried to wedge it in front of the door. But he knew it wouldn't be enough. He pushed the table to add extra weight, and began frantically looking around the room for something else to help. Some way out. Some way to stop it. But there was nothing. Alan clutched the little alarm clock and screamed at it. "WAKE UP!"

"SEVEN," said the creature outside, headlamp eyes still intent on the keypad. Beep.

Alan was going to die. With sagging shoulders, he slumped to the floor and buried his head in his hands. What could he do?

"Wake up," he pleaded to the alarm clock. But it just glared at him with that same time in red digits. 3:33am.

"FOUR." Beep.

Alan's eyes fell on the notebook, pages spread out lopsided. He could warn Dr Hampsell. Tell her that it saw her. That somehow that meant it knew the same things she did. Snatching up pencil and notepad, Alan began to scrawl out a warning, but the pencil left no marks. He tried carving it into the floor, but he couldn't scratch anything into the concrete surface. It needed time, he remembered.

"Nothing works in here," Alan whispered to himself, "Nothing works except for me."

There was another form of ink he could use. A desperate, final sort of ink. Alan gripped the pencil and placed the graphite point against the veins of his forearm. Raising it high, and bracing to plunge it down, Alan took a deep breath as he prepared to slice himself open. But before he could muster the courage, the creature outside spoke one final time.

"NINE."

Beep.

Alan had thought that those beeps were the worst sound he had ever heard. But the melodic chime of the Containment Cell door opening took that honour. The door itself only opened a haircrack. A slither. But that was enough.

When Alan looked up at the door, his view was blocked.

***

Lights returned as though nothing had happened. The door continued swinging open, pushing Alan's makeshift blockade with it.

Containment Cell 333 had a modest interior. A small bedside table, tipped over. A single bed; flipped and propped up behind the door. Bedsheets sprawled across the floor. A silver alarm clock. And that was it. No Alan Pierson. No pencil he had been planning to open his veins with. Nothing much at all, really.

Although, to anyone looking closely enough, there was a man in a red leather armchair. He was sat in the far corner of the room, pushed tightly up against the glass, leaning down and intently examining a book on his lap. He traced the words with a finger, frowning, before flicking back and forth. Back and forth.

"Strange," said The Narrator, "seems to be a page missing."

He licked a finger and rubbed at the edges of the pages, trying to separate them, but there was simply nothing there.

Footsteps trotted down the hallway, and when Dr Hampsell stepped in sight of the empty Cell, she screamed. The glass of water in her hand tumbled to the ground and shattered.

The Narrator casually turned in his seat to see the commotion, before tutting. The alarm clock in the room said the time was 3:34am. The watch on Dr Hampsell's wrist disagreed. 3:35am, it claimed.

"Terrible shame," The Narrator muttered. "One minute

fast."

Dr Hampsell desperately searched down the corridors, screaming Alan's name, her voice growing increasingly shrill and panicked.

The Narrator watched her, shaking his head. "I do hope she doesn't blame herself too badly," he said, idly flicking through the pages of his book. After a moment he stopped, and traced the words on a page near the end. "Ah," he said. "Oh dear."

Snapping the book shut, he placed it back on his shelf and nibbled on a biscuit. His eyes watched the shifting books swell and shrink. With fingers raised, he waited, poised and ready to strike. Leaning intently forwards in his seat, his hand darted out like a viper, lightning fast, snatching up a tiny, crumbled brown envelope.

"Blaming yourself when disaster strikes is natural," he said, drawing a finger across the torn edges of the envelope. He reached inside, and drew out a folded piece of paper. The scribbled words across its surface looked handwritten. The Narrator unfolded it and smiled to himself. "Blaming others though? That's much more fun."

# "Yours Artificially"

*[ copy of letter sent to CEO of Schmitt Robotics ]*

Dear Fredrich,

I do hope you open this particular letter. Despite what you might be expecting, I wish to thank you.

If you cast your mind back all those years ago, when you closed our project down and announced there would be no further funding, I did perhaps not handle it with grace or humility. In fact, I quite recall I grovelled! To the alarm and dismay of my colleagues, I do believe I clutched at your trouser legs and wept. I made quite the fool of myself, no doubt. But at that time I did not see the larger picture. I only saw the lack of resources, loss of personnel and the shattering fragment of my soul that hoped for a better future. I did not realise the inspiration and drive that little act of yours would provide me. You lit quite the fire inside me, Fredrich. And it would appear there are few motivators as powerful as raw, burning hatred.

"No progress", was what you claimed. "An impossible task", you firmly stated.

I watched them turn off my children one by one. Torn apart and sold for scrap. You never saw them as anything more than simple machines, but I did. I felt the snip of every cable. The snap of every circuit. And if you and your suited ilk saw me as obsessive before, it would have made your skin crawl to see what I became after that day. After the death of my children.

Yet as fortune would have it, you didn't get them all. You only killed the ones I showed you. My prototypes and unfinished works survived. And although I had lost my team, although I no longer had your spacious workshops or bountiful resources, I began to rebuild. Without your borrowed power, I was forced to improvise. Necessity, as they say, is the mother of invention.

How many times did I tell you, Fredrich? We were going about it all wrong. To build a mind of metal and expect it to think? As well teach dust to sing. No, no, no. In order to think, you must feel. And what is the only composite material in the universe that can feel?

Flesh.

Only flesh can truly feel. We can simulate nerves in a machine, teach it to scream and recoil, but it does not truly feel pain, merely an impression of pain. It is an act. A sham. An illusion made only to fool ourselves. The machine simply does what it is told. There is no freedom in that. No thought.

How can a computer feel, if we do not give it skin?

My first experiment sought to change this. But I cannot make flesh. Not yet. No, for now I have to simply borrow it. Nobody missed the donor. Nobody even noticed he was gone. But he asked for change, and I certainly gave it to him.

Did you know that a brain transplant has another name? They also call it a 'full-body transplant', as technically - to the operatee, at least - it is the body that swaps. Not the brain. Interesting, I'm sure you'll agree. The donor didn't seem to grasp the concept. It hardly mattered, his brain wasn't the part I was interested in. The body was considerably neglected, but it sufficed, and I imagined it would be appreciated much more by a new mind. So I set to work. Removed the organic brain, replacing it with a digital mind. Grafting cranial nerves to the circuit boards was the challenge; such finicky work. Not to mention melting nervous tissue and a soldering iron make for a truly acrid combination. I could smell it in my clothes and hair for days after the procedure.

Alas, the grafting process caused too much scarring, and the data transfer was... limited. My carefully crafted machine mind did little more than scream in its brand new body. Just lay there, screaming until its vocal chords twanged apart and the only sound it could emit was a bubbling rasp. An unexpected curiosity was that it refused to die. Blood flow is needed to sustain a living brain, but not a computer. Everything still functioned, at least in some capacity. Even as I unplugged wires and severed nerves, somehow it still kept making that same rasp, its eyes following me as I tried, in vain, to switch it off.

My error was apparent. I had created a mind that could feel, but not think. And upon this realisation, I heard an echo of your voice. "The brain has two sides, the left and the right."

Do you remember, Fredrich? Oh, but you must. I was your right sided brain. All expression, imagination and feeling. Gunderson was your left sided brain. All logic, analysis and facts. Together, we made the perfect pair. I know you remember, Fredrich. You said it so often. But that wasn't the only echo of your voice that inspired my next experiment. Do you remember what else you would tell me, what else you would mutter when Gunderson left the room?

"He has a mind like a calculator, that one."

I'm sure you can imagine where that train of thought sent me. Gunderson was easy enough to acquire. Much like myself, he was too obsessed with his work to ever truly walk away. The promise of a breakthrough was enough to obtain the crucial piece of equipment I needed. Gunderson's mind.

We're more akin to machines than we like to admit. Conscious thought is merely a combination of neurons firing on or off. Gunderson was fluent in English and German, but his brain spoke binary. Instead of 'one', his neurons flared up, screaming. Instead of 'zero', they went cold. Translating was easy, inserting needle probes into the precise locations necessary for communication was the challenge. Once you get the hang of it though, the human body is simply another machine. Veins are our wires. Blood, our electricity. Nerves carry information at lightning speeds, and yet we are so... clumsy compared to our digital children.

Gunderson realised this when he awoke. If he had a mind like a calculator before, he had just experienced a quantum upgrade. He was no longer limited by flesh. No longer bound by meat. He answered every question set to him in imperceptible fractions of a nanosecond. He breezed through the Turing Test. His memories were intact, and retrievable to astonishing clarity. If I requested information on a specific date of our shared history, he would know what filling I had in my sandwich, what the weather was like and what we had achieved that day. Perfect recall. Beyond perfect.

He would also ask questions of his own.

[ why? ] was a common one that would flicker upon his black screen. Those square brackets always enclosed his inner thoughts, although they were not programmed by me. I gain some small comfort in believing they were Gunderson's own choice. Some internal desire to be organised, and clear in his communication. He always was efficient, wasn't he?

[ why? ] he would ask in glowing green letters.

[ why? ]

[ why? ]

[ why? ]

He never showed anger at my betrayal. Never displayed joy at his newfound processing speeds. No sadness for the loss of his body. No sorrow. No hate. No love. No feeling at all.

After his questions went unanswered for long enough, he seemed to accept he would get no answer from me, and even went as far as suggesting ways I could optimise the cruel procedure I had performed on him.

[ needle seventy-two requires adjustment ] would blink onto his screen. Cold. Emotionless. And though I followed his instructions, and though he was correct every time, I knew this was just another failed experiment. Just another set back.

This time, I had made a machine that could think, but not feel.

[ what is my name? ] it asked.

"Gunderson", I replied.

[ before, yes. but different now. ]

"You've been promoted," I told it. "That joke we had, do you remember?"

[ 'keep working this hard, and you'll never be promoted to management.' i remember. ]

"Well, congratulations, you've been promoted."

[ do not understand. what is my name? ]

"MANAGEMENT."

It remembered the joke, but maintained none of the humour. It was a soulless husk. Imitation again. Worse than the first. It angered me.

I carted it out into the wilderness with just a battery pack for company. Left it out there in the cold, bleak landscape. Wind tore against its plastic moulding, and I stuffed the brain inside to join the circuitry. It was late when I finally trudged away. Snow fell gently from the sky, and I turned back to look at my creation. Against the black night sky, the blizzard looked like television static. Yet despite all its intelligence, the little machine at its centre had no clue what was even happening. It could not feel the chill. Could not appreciate the silence of the blanketing snow. Did not realise I had abandoned it. It didn't even know it was dark. And as the snow settled above its vents and began to melt, dripping onto its electrical organs, it had no idea it was about to die.

If I had dragged a child out into the woods, they would have known. They would have cried and called out for aid. They would have -

Oh, I'm sorry Fredrich. I didn't think. To mention children in such a manner, after the recent disappearance of your boy. Insensitive of me. Inconsiderate. Monstrous.

After all, I know first hand how it feels to have your children wrenched away from you. Before they had reached their true potential. Before they had even begun to blossom. I know that paralysing powerlessness. How it grasps your throat and refuses to let go. Unfortunately, should the worst happen - as it did to me, I might remind you - that sensation never truly leaves.

At the start of this letter, I wished to thank you, and I'm sure you're wondering why. My two experiments failed. But that is how we learn, isn't it Fredrich? Through failure! We don't terminate a project halfway through, we dust ourselves off and try again!

So, I had created one mind that could feel and not think. Another that could think and not feel. Somewhere between the two must hold the key, I proposed. My experiments continued, with renewed effort and wild creativity. But every. Single. One. Failed.

But then I saw you. You and your boy, with big, beaming smiles. Adorning my television screen like digital prophets. Your hand resting tenderly on his shoulder, your voice like rusty nails upon my soul.

"Children," you said proudly. "Children are the key to the future."

How right you were, Fredrich. Their minds are so much more malleable. Adult minds are too far gone, too bound by this reality. They cannot bend or flex without shattering. But your boy's? Clay within my hand.

So, thank you Fredrich. You have shown me the key to unlocking the digital mind, and as thanks, I return him to you, unharmed.

I'm sure an eye for detail such as yours will have noted the FDD enclosed within the envelope of this letter. 'Floppy discs', I believe they are being called now. The name always bemused me. Machines are not floppy, but we are!

Your boy certainly was. But not to worry. I've straightened all his edges. There wasn't much data to process, as it happens. Not as many memories as Gunderson, or as much brain power. And with the lessons I've learned since you fired me, I've become much more efficient. You'll find his entire mind on that little black disc, compressed down to a mere 6kb.

Unlike Gunderson, your boy can still feel. He'll type a little '@' if he's angry, or '#' if he's in pain. ';' when he's sad, or '+' when he's hungry. It's all in the manual. That's on there too. Just plug it in, and have a play around. I'm sure a man of your calibre can figure it out.

I won't keep you. I'm sure you and your boy have a lot of catching up to do. Such a shame I can't do the same with my children.

Thanks again, Fredrich. For everything.

Yours artificially,
Josef Harkreft

# Item 000
# [MANAGEMENT]

< information missing >

# Item 000

Dark columns of machinery hummed with incessant spinning fans, diodes blinking on and off, thick bunches of wires running along the walls. Despite being swollen to bursting with computer equipment, there was a certain subtle order to Cell 000. Equipment was centralised in neat rows, arranged in size order. One item broke this self-imposed rule; a small and archaic looking computer, placed on a two-tier shelf trolley. It sat within the centre of the cell, with hundreds of trailing cables connected into the back of the small machine. Its screen and keyboard were all a single piece within its plastic moulded, cream coloured shell.

Upon its black screen, words flickered and disappeared before any human eye could read them. Commands. Functions. Processes. All logged and filed within the hidden depths of this tiny computer. Underneath the flickering text, a glowing green underscore blinked, ready for input.

Two fingers pressed onto the keyboard of Item 000, and began to impersonate a pair of miniature legs walking across, jabbing random keys with their fingertip feet. Corresponding gibberish began to type on the screen, and in response the computer flared up numerous security warnings. The Narrator smiled to himself.

"Here we are. The big brain of Floor Fifty-Four. Or is it the beating heart? Vitals organs are always so confusing and..." The Narrator made absent grasping motions with his hands, "squishy."

Around the room, cameras and sensors whirred, trying in vain to detect whatever presence was inside. Lenses pointed directly at The Narrator, clicking faintly as they switched through thermal imaging, hyperspectral imagery and structured light scanners, all to no avail. No matter how they looked, the cameras only showed an empty room. The Narrator gave a leisurely wave at each in turn.

"Yes, a happy ending for once, the little computer survived. And my my, look how it's grown!" The Narrator gestured around the room, eyeing the sleek boxes of machinery. "What big teeth you have."

Placing his crumpled letter back inside the envelope, The Narrator casually reached over to his shifting shelf and tucked it between two books. Then he turned his attention to the little cream computer. It looked archaic, surrounded by its modern contemporary descendants, and the maze of wires and adapters connected into its small back panel somehow made it look even smaller. Yes despite its age and stature, there was a certain undeniable power to the little machine. Something unsensed that pulsed and jittered.

"The story said it had a brain," mused The Narrator, unscrewing a square side panel with a fingernail. The tiny door swung open, revealing the inner circuit boards and a small tangle of wires. "But I suppose you can't believe everything you read."

As he closed the door, his eyes lingered on a stain around the sharp edges of a resistor. A vaguely organic-looking stain. "Ah," he said, nodding. "*Had*. It *had* a brain. You see? I did tell you words were important."

Placing a hand on top of the little computer's cream monitor, The Narrator drummed his fingers thoughtfully. "Me and this little fellow have known each other quite some time. Not friends, perhaps, but... neighbours? Cellmates? Rivals?"

Removing his hand, The Narrator shrugged and scooped up

his nearby cup.

“Technically, I was the first Item of Interest on Floor Fifty-Four. Yet this little machine still claims to precede me. It boils down to that age old question - which came first, the chicken or the egg? The prisoner, or the prison guard?”

The Narrator sipped his tea, before wincing and looking at the china cup aghast.

“Cold already. I do apologise. It seems I have committed the cardinal sin of storytelling. I have been rambling.” The Narrator poured the dregs of his cup onto a nearby server, which sizzled and sparked as the liquid seeped through its vents. “I promised you the beginning of Floor Fifty-Four, didn’t I? Well, fortunately enough, we’re in the right place.”

The Narrator slapped the top of Item 000, making its screen blink furiously.

“It was all this one’s idea, wasn’t it?” he cooed.

In glowing green font, frantic instructions appeared upon the screen of Item 000.

[ EXTERNAL FORCE DETECTED ]

[ RECOMMENDED: INSPECTION OF CELL 000 ]

[ AUTHORISED: TOP PRIORITY ]

As tendrils of smoke began to snake out of the screw holes of the nearby server, The Narrator collected a thick instruction manual from his shelf. Holding it outstretched, he blew off a thick layer of dust and cobwebs, before placing it on his lap and reading its pages.

***

With an enthusiastic ping, heavy elevator doors slid apart, revealing two smartly dressed gentlemen and a two-tier shelf trolley.

“I didn’t know the elevator went down this low,” mused the first, rubbing finger and thumb across his moustache, which was just beginning to show flecks of grey amongst the mousy brown.

“It didn’t,” said the other, stepping out into the dim concrete corridor. His suit was impeccably pressed, without a single visible crease. The way he held his back and shoulders made it appear as though he could support the weight of the world, if required. Even his sure-footed strides spoke of a quiet certainty. “The Ministers only approved it today.”

Pushing the trolley and its contents - a small cream computer - out into the corridor, the first man shot an uneasy glance at his companion. “And how was that, Edgar? Meeting the Ministers?”

Edgar’s confident strides didn’t falter. “About as unsettling as you might expect,” he said, aiming a smirk over his shoulder. As the two men came to a junction in the corridor, splitting off in three directions, Edgar continued ahead without a sideways look. “This way, Radford.”

Although his companion never spared a glance for his surroundings, Radford did. All three options appeared the same - short corridors with dead ends, surrounded on all sides by empty glass-fronted rooms. As they continued on their path, Radford got a better look at these rooms. Plain and empty, with a subtle doorway into each. It reminded Radford of an aquarium, drained of all water and life. As for its intended purpose, he had some guesses. “Is this place going to be a museum?” he asked with a raised eyebrow, “Or a prison?”

“Both,” said Edgar, as they passed empty room after empty room. All the while, the wheels of the trolley squeaked excitedly. “And more.”

Rather quickly, they ran out of corridor to walk down, and Edgar placed the palm of his hand onto a panel near the final room. Vivid blue light illuminated Edgar's hand, and a melodic jingle rang out as the door to the cell swung inward.

"It's going to be much smaller than Floor Nine," said Edgar. "More humble."

He motioned inside the open doorway, and Radford pushed the trolley inside the room.

"Seems like a big change of pace," Radford said, maneuvering the trolley into the centre of the room and adjusting it until the computer faced the glass wall, looking out to the corridor. "Just here?"

"That's perfect," said Edgar.

Radford let go of the trolley and straightened to look at his companion. "You didn't bring me here just to shift this computer, did you?"

"Perceptive as ever," Edgar replied with a smile. "I need an Agent. A good one."

"You need an Agent..." repeated Radford, chewing on the words before his eyes grew wide. "Edgar, have they made you Chairman?"

A broad grin spread across Edgar's face. "Floor Fifty-Four doesn't officially exist yet. But once it does, yes. I will be Chairman 54. I was hoping you would do the honours."

Radford shook his head in astonishment. "I can't - I don't have the authority to-"

"That's where this little computer comes in. He's going to help me run things. It's all pre-approved. Everything ready to deploy. It just needs someone to press 'enter'."

Radford blinked the shock from his eyes, and glanced down at the little computer. Just as Edgar claimed, burning in glowing green font upon the screen were the words *[COMMENCE DEPLOYMENT OF FLOOR FIFTY-FOUR]*, above a vertical line that flickered expectantly for input.

"But - why me?"

"Because I wanted you to know you're my first choice. And what better way to prove it, than to have you deliver this here? Than to have you press the button that makes it real."

"No, I mean... why me?"

"Oh, come on Rupert. I'm not going to stand here and flatter you. Primarily, I chose you because you're best suited for the job. Secondly, I want to work with someone I can stand. Lastly, we both know Floor Nine is a young man's game. I've seen - and felt - what that place does to people."

Fingers that had been reaching for the keyboard fell to Radford's side. His moustache bristled. "So I'm a pity-hire? You're saving me from hellfire and brimstone. Is that all this place is... An easy retirement?"

Edgar laughed. "Hardly. We'll be building a new Floor from scratch. And if this computer is to be believed, we're about to experience an exponential growth of the strange and inexplicable. Humanity is more connected than ever, our cultures and histories intertwining. Overlapping. Technology is exploding in ways even the boys on Floor Nineteen could never have predicted... Not to mention the days of Empire are crumbling, if they've not already collapsed entirely. The world is changing, Radford. And I need you to help keep it sane."

Edgar placed a hand on Radford's shoulder. "So, no," he continued, "this isn't an 'easy retirement'. The fact that would put you off is the reason you're here. The Ministry of Secrets has created stability and control for over a hundred years. All the Gods are entombed, all the monsters are registered, all the magic extinguished. But whatever is happening now, it's...

something different. It's not something we can easily define, or categorise, or control. Anomalies, they're calling them."

"Anomalies," repeated Radford, tasting the word on his tongue and running a finger and thumb across his moustache. "Well, now I know I'm getting old."

"We both are," agreed Edgar. "But name me one thing in this entire Ministry that isn't older..."

Radford nodded sagely, before a smile etched itself onto his face. He pointed at the computer in front of him. "This little thing. Only a few years old, surely?"

Now both men smiled. Edgar clapped his hands together. "Exactly! This whole Ministry is full to the brim with remnants of the old world. But this Floor? Everything inside will be from some new world we can't see yet. Some new world that's still being born..." Edgar paced up to the glass, gazing out at the empty corridor outside. "How did you feel Rupert, the first time you saw Hell?"

Radford's eyes found the ground, and stayed there. "Small," he said, finally.

"Powerless," agreed Edgar, hands clasped behind his back. "Insignificant. That's how I felt. Like we were all just playthings for cruel, uncaring Gods. But that's not true any more, is it?" His gesture took in the whole structure around them, and every layer above. He turned, his eyes dancing. "We're not their playthings now. I've seen their cages. Anubis. Zeus. Loki. Give it another millennia or two, and who knows, humanity may start looking a little bit like Gods themselves."

"This is all starting to sound a bit above my pay-grade," said Radford, shaking his head.

"Forgive me, I just get excited," said Edgar, placing a hand on the monitor of the little computer. "A new frontier, Radford.

One that seems largely man-made. All those Fifty-Three Floors above us, combining, fusing together with mankind to make things we've never seen before. And we'll be here, to make sure that isn't unleashed on an unsuspecting world."

"All that, down here eh?" Radford asked, sceptically looking down the short, empty corridor. "Just me and you, doing all that?"

"At first," said Edgar, pressing a button to open the cell door. "Assuming you 'cut the ribbon', that is." Without another glance, he left the room, and stepped outside.

Alone with the computer, Radford stared down at its little screen. Green text flicked across the top, but the same words still glowed above the input cursor.

*[COMMENCE DEPLOYMENT OF FLOOR FIFTY-FOUR]*

All Radford had to do was push the button. Or leave. The door to the cell was still wide open. He could even see the Astral Elevator, glinting at him from down the hall.

He knew that if he left, Edgar wouldn't stop him. Wouldn't try to convince him. Likely would never mention it again. Edgar would find someone else, become Chairman 54, and disappear completely. Radford would stay on Floor Nine, fishing souls out of Hell's gutters until he grew too old to do it properly. How many days until that fate came true?

"Fuck it," said Radford, and pressed the enter key. With those words, Floor Fifty-Four was born. There were no fireworks. No curtains parted. Not even a rumble of thunder from unseen skies. The green text simply flickered away, replaced with rapidly scrolling text blinking far too fast to be read.

Waiting for a moment to see if anything else happened - it didn't - Radford walked through the open door and joined

Edgar in the hall. When Edgar didn't say anything, Radford filled the silence.

"I've done it."

"I know."

For all his excitement and speculation before, now the deed was done, it was hard to get a read on Edgar at all. No emotion on his face, no difference in his body language. For a man who seemed to love the sound of his own voice, Radford wished Edgar would say something now. Once again, he found himself speaking up to replace the void.

"All these empty cells," said Radford, sweeping his eyes up and down the corridor ahead. "What else are you putting inside them?"

Edgar smiled. "Management has been recommending certain item relocations for some time. In total, we have twenty eight other items that are due for transfer here. The rest? Out there in the big wide world, just waiting to be found, apparently. We have some leads, and more seem to crop up every day. Management predicts that in fifty years time, we'll have a thousand items down here."

"I guess we've got our work cut out for us."

"Well, you know what they say. Build it..." Edgar nodded over Radford's shoulder, "and they shall come."

Radford turned to the formerly empty cell behind him, and instead came face-to-face with a well dressed man in a red leather chair. Sat comfortably behind the glass, the man looked up from the book in his hands and flashed a pleasant smile.

A silver revolver sprang from its holster on Radford's leg. It leapt into the air and found itself nestled inside Radford's palm. In the blink of an eye, the barrel was pointing at this strange man's head, as Radford's other hand outstretched to push Edgar back to safety.

"Relax, Rupert." Edgar stepped around Radford's offer of protection and strode upto the glass, hands stuffed inside his trouser pockets. "I'm sure if he wanted to hurt us, he'd have appeared closer, and wouldn't be reading a book. Besides, your bullets won't do much good against this stuff." He tapped the glass, and turned to the stranger inside. "Hello there. And who might you be?"

The Narrator smiled, as warm as fresh apple crumble. "Oh, don't mind me. I'm just showing them around. Letting them get a feel for the place."

"We weren't expecting guests," said Edgar, looking around the empty corridors. "I'd offer you a tour, but there's really not much to see."

Snapping his book shut with an echo that bounced around the walls, The Narrator rested the volume on the arm of his chair, and took the last biscuit from his plate. He raised it to his teeth.

"Sir..." began Radford quietly, weapon still trained on the figure inside the cell, "are you sure this is-"

Edgar replied with a gesture to lower the gun, never taking his eyes away from The Narrator. His smile never slipped, his posture never faltered.

"I'd never hurt you, Agent Radford..." The Narrator said, taking a bite out of his biscuit. Beside him, his bookshelf began to swell, cramming itself so full with books that the spines began to bulge. "If I did, I'd have nothing to read."

Still keeping his eyes on the strange man, Edgar slowly began nodding to himself. His smile widened, and soon he began to look almost as smug as The Narrator himself. "You're fourth dimensional, aren't you?"

Taking another bite of his biscuit, The Narrator chewed slowly. Finally, once he had swallowed the last morsel, he said, "My, my. What a *clever* little boy you are Eddie."

That did make Edgar's smile slip. Those were the words his mother would scold him with as a child. The exact same intonation. That familiar, barely concealed venom.

"He experiences time differently to us," said Edgar, turning to his colleague. "Any information we reveal to him in the future, he will know right now."

Agent Radford finally lowered his revolver, holstering it before moving up to the cell. "You've encountered something like this before?"

"Never like this. I'm not aware of anything like... this."

Inside his cell, The Narrator's eyes shimmered.

"Although, I suppose it bodes well for our..." Edgar shot a glance at the computer in the adjacent cell. "...joint venture."

"Because if he's here now," Radford began slowly, brushing his moustache with a finger and thumb, "it implies this place holds future significance?"

Edgar nodded, and walked up to the glass of The Narrator's cell, getting so close his breath steamed up on the surface. "Welcome to Floor Fifty-Four, I suppose. We weren't expecting items to appear spontaneously, or voluntarily. What do you want, exactly?"

The Narrator made a show of looking over his shoulders, before pointing to himself in mock surprise. "Me? I wouldn't say no to a cup of tea. Perhaps some more biscuits." He rattled his empty plate before adding, "Nice ones."

# Adieu

Fifty years later, The Narrator closed the book in his lap. He looked astonishingly good for his age. No different, in fact. Not a single extra white hair in the fifty years he'd just travelled.

His chair was no more sun-bleached, there were no extra scuffs on the timber legs. Not so much as a paper scratch on the bookshelf, and his books - when they stopped still long enough to see them - looked exactly as they always had. Some were box-fresh, the ink barely dry. Some looked like they'd been taken to a library and beaten up, all dog-eared with pages torn from the spine. But that was how they'd always looked.

No, the only thing that had changed in fifty years was his surroundings. Instead of cold concrete, his chair sat atop rich oak floorboards which gleamed in the warm light of the fireplace. Instead of bare and sterile walls, pristine wallpaper enveloped the room like some luxurious gift-wrapped present, gild-framed artwork hanging proudly. Where harsh overhead lighting had been before, a golden chandelier now glittered and twinkled.

And, although it could not be seen from this room, even The Narrator's neighbours had changed. Item 000 had been moved far, far away. Instead of empty cells, all the immediately adjacent rooms were purpose built. A little tea room, shelves teeming with every variety of biscuit. A small gallery, hosting different masterpieces for when The Narrator wanted something new to decorate his walls. A secret observation room that the scientists hoped The Narrator didn't know about, but obviously did. The same observation room that was mysteriously malfunctioning today, whilst The Narrator addressed the air with a coy smile.

"Well, there we have it. I promised you a dipping of the toe into unfamiliar waters, and by now I'm sure your feet are sufficiently moist. But much like the oceans themselves, you can always go deeper, should you dare."

Reaching over to place his book on the shelf, the Narrator lingered above the tray, with the empty cup and not-quite-empty plate. Spying an extra morsel of broken biscuit, he snatched up the plate.

"At the very start of our time together, you heard Doctor Milton ask why I stayed. Why, if I can go anywhere, see anything... Then why am I still here, deep within Floor Fifty-Four, patiently waiting inside these walls?"

He gathered the last crums of biscuit, sprinkling it into his gaping maw, before settling the plate back down on the tray along with the empty cup.

"As I said, a dull question. The real question, of course, surrounded by stories as I am..." He smiled wider than he ever had. His cheeks bulged with it, and his open armed gesture took in the world. "Why would I ever leave?"

From outside, there drifted a melodic beeping, followed by a hydraulic hiss as the black door swung open. This time it was a solitary guard who entered. He still clutched his weapon, but there was no visible intent to use it.

The man who was not a man ceased his conversation with the air, and shot a pleasant smile at the guard.

"Good evening Jason. I must say, you're looking rather tired, old chap. Not sleeping well?"

Black boots stepped closer, keeping a respectable distance behind the line. The guard nodded glumly and held out an expectant hand. “You could say that.”

“Something on your mind, Jason?”

“Nope. Pass me the tray, please.”

“Nothing at all...?”

“No. Pass me the tray.”

The tray remained on its table, safely nestled within the boundary painted by the line on the floor. The Narrator smiled warmly, his cheeks stretching.

“Not your wife? Not Rebecca?”

The guard’s outstretched hand dropped. His entire body slumped, shoulders sagging, face drooping, arm falling limp to his side. His mouth worked uselessly, and all the while, The Narrator watched him with that same smile.

“Wh- How do you- How do you know about her?” stammered Jason, his lips quivering and turning white as the guard leveled an accusing finger at the man on the chair.

Removing his half moon glasses, the man who was not a man studied his bookshelf, the smile replaced by a look of false concern.

“I found the chapter in the hospital particularly tragic. I really am sorry, Jason,” his fingers tapped the spines of the books, the colours and titles flickering at his touch. “All this time you wasted in this place, trying to build a better life for the three of you. But now it’s just two, isn’t it Jason? Perhaps soon, only one.”

As he made tutting noises, his searching fingers at last found the book they were looking for, and he retrieved it from his shelves. Flicking through the pages, occasionally licking a single finger, he muttered to himself. “Now where were we, where were we...?”

Jason searched over his shoulder, as if hoping he might see

someone, as if hoping this was all a game, a joke, a ploy, that someone was about to shake him loose from. There was nobody there. Just the man who was not a man. Just his many, many books.

"Ah!" said The Narrator suddenly, making Jason flinch. "Yes, a sleepless night. Lying in your cramped mattress in the guard's quarters, listening to Bryce snore, listening to the leaky tap drip, drip, drip. All the while staring at that stain on the ceiling, all the while wondering if she'll still be alive when you finish this stint. How many days are left now Jason? Ah, it says here, thirteen. Just thirteen days until you're allowed back to the surface. But will Rebecca still be there? Hmm..."

If there had ever been any colour in Jason's face, it was long gone now. With unblinking eyes, he stared at the man, at his book. Jason's lips trembled, but no words came out. The silence seemed to draw the man's attention from the pages of his book.

"We could always... skip ahead? Rather naughty, but we've all done it haven't we?" He flashed a sickly smile at Jason.

"It says here that you simply take the tray and leave, but..." he made a point of turning to the tray, still untouched on the table. "Ah, no. Here we are. The words are changing now."

"You're lying," managed Jason. If he'd meant it to sound defiant, nobody would have known.

"That's what it says you say," said The Narrator, pointing to a line in his book. "Right here..." He began to read the pages of his book aloud, finger tracing along the words. "*'You're lying, said Jason. If he'd meant it to sound defiant, nobody would have known.'* See?" The man turned his book around and offered it to Jason.

For a moment, Jason's hands drifted towards the book, but then he paused. His eyes focused on the line on the ground, just beyond the toe of his boots. It was there for a reason. It was there to protect him. Jason knew he was not supposed to step beyond that line. Jason knew he was not supposed to touch the man who was not a man.

“They’re just words,” said The Narrator, shaking the book and leaning almost painfully out of his leather chair. “Words can’t hurt you. Sticks and stones, and so on...”

The Narrator turned towards empty space, and winked. Jason did not see. His eyes were fixated on the book before him. A book which was describing him looking at its pages, desperate to discover the fate of his wife. His every action described before it happened, his every thought appearing as words on the page, before they even entered his mind.

Jason’s legs couldn’t hold him any more, and he dropped to his knees, like the book said he would. He desperately tore through the pages, skipping ahead, skipping ahead.

In a plump, red leather armchair, wrapped in a chequered three-piece suit, a man who was not a man at all made a shooing gesture at the air, towards the open door.

***

In the twisting maze of Floor Fifty-Four, sirens wailed their mournful song. The cold corridor was awash with swirling red lights. Black boots stomped across the concrete floor, running towards a windowless room with an open, black door.

“Jason!” shouted someone, sprinting with sizzling weapons grasped in hand. “Get away from him Jason!”

Bodies piled into the chamber, which had thick black text above the door frame. Words which read:

## *Item 001*
## *"The Narrator"*

The corridors seemed to stretch on forever, surrounded on both sides by row after row of glass-fronted cells. Something different watched from inside every box. Each occupant stranger than the last. Dozens of them. Hundreds. More.

Jason was dragged out from the hungry mouth of Cell 001, screaming nonsense. He still gripped the book in his hands. The book which told the story of his own life. The heavy black door of Chamber 001 was thrown shut. Electronically bolted and sealed tight.

Locked, once more.

For now.

**Item 001**
**"THE NARRATOR"**

[appeared spontaneously during formation of Floor Fifty-Four]

# THE END

But it doesn't need to be.

There are hundreds of horrors on Floor Fifty-Four.
Each has a story to tell.
Some have entire scientific reports.

Item 020 - "Oodoov"
Item 303 - "Abigail"
Item 042 - "Two-seater"
Item 210 - "Copycat"
Item 333 - "25-Hour Clock"
Item 000 - [management]

Floor Fifty-Four is still growing.
Each month, something new joins the floor.



Keep reading for an exclusive tease of the next book from
FLOOR FIFTY-FOUR.

COMING SOON - The first big case for Agent Radford in his new role on Floor Fifty-Four. People are going missing on the Yorkshire Moors. When the lead suspect - a local vampire - proves innocent, Radford is caught up in a race against time to catch the real killer. Guilt is not a requirement for the brutal guards of Floor Thirty - a government prison for monsters - and the innocent vampire's life becomes Radford's to save.

## **MIDNIGHT CALLER - PREVIEW**

# Yorkshire. 1988.

It was cold on the moors, cold enough to make the grass shiver. Deep amongst the swaying blades, a man called Graham Kett was taking his final steps. He had no idea of course, but then few ever do.

"Stupid bloody thing," he muttered, fiddling with his faulty headlamp. His twitching fingers cast elongated shadows across the dark, bristling field. Even the moon had abandoned him now, lost behind unseen clouds. The path he'd been trying to follow had long since faded away, and Graham knew it would be best to turn back.

He twisted in the darkness. If only he knew which way back was. If only his flickering headlamp would let him see further than he could spit, maybe he'd catch a glimpse of trees, or hedgerows, or stone walls; anything to help him orientate himself. Still, it wasn't like the field could go on forever...

Gritting his teeth and steeling himself against the winter winds - made worse by bitter nightfall - Graham trudged forward. His wife had been right. It *was* too late to go out. He *had* gotten lost. But he'd take any lecture she'd prepared if it meant a warm bed and some rest.

The dog lead went taught in his hands, and Graham stopped dead.

"What's wrong with you now?" he called over his shoulder, exasperated. He couldn't even see Watson. Giving the lead a gentle tug, he hoped the Alsatian would catch up. No such luck. Now he'd even lost the bloody dog. Graham sighed. Using the lead to guide his hand, he tracked back, step by step, until it vanished down into the thick grass.

"Watson?" he asked, parting the grass, struggling to see in what dim light the headlamp provided.

His hands found fur, and he crouched down to pet the dog.

Watson was laid down, head resting on his paws, refusing to move. He looked up at Graham with pitiful eyes. As Graham's fingers scratched behind his ears, the dog tilted his head, never saying no to a fuss.

"Sulking, are you?" muttered Graham, giving the lead a more insistent tug and forcing Watson to stand. "Too dark, or too cold?"

The wind dug into the gaps between Graham's clothes, seeming to seek out his skin. He shuddered and wrapped his arms tightly around his chest. "Or both..." he whispered to himself.

Graham started moving, squinting into the distance. Barely visible amongst the black canvas was a small, soft light. Though he was too far away to make it out, any light was welcome in his current situation. If it was a house - or anything at all, really - there should be a path leading to it. A path Graham could follow and figure out where he'd ended up.

Turning towards it, the lead caught in his hands again, almost yanking his arm out his socket. Once again, the dog had laid down.

"Come on!" said Graham, tugging the lead, growing increasingly frustrated at Watson. This walk was supposed to be for his benefit after all. "Daft sod," muttered Graham.

As they began to make headway, Graham still couldn't make out the source of the light, but could now hear a faint, distant sound. His ears strained to make it out against the rustling grass. But it sounded like… ringing.

The quiet ringing of a telephone.

Hope rising in his chest, Graham quickened his pace, the ringing growing steadily louder with each step. As he got closer, he saw hedgerows, the pinprick of light shining just beyond them.

He stalked around them until he found a gap. The ringing telephone was now so loud, it drowned out the wind. As Graham's boots left the grass and found hard gravel, they slipped. Watson had planted his feet, sending Graham reeling around and colliding to the ground.

Wiping muck from his hands and reaching to the very depths of his patience, Graham clambered up and stroked the dog's back. Between each screeching ring, he could hear the dog's soft whimpers. Graham supposed the noise would be even louder to the dog.

"It's alright," he said soothingly, "come on."

They'd found the path, now he just needed to decide which way to go. Turning to assess, Graham's eyes fell on the long, sleek shape of a telephone box, not twenty metres away. Deep crimson, filled with thick glass panels from top to bottom, it's internal lighting casting a reddish gloom over the path. It looked amiss amongst the darkness, amongst the rolling hills and bristling leaves. The ringing noise had grown so loud, Graham's whole body tensed up with each ring, as though the decibels were piercing beneath his flesh, as though the phone were calling to him, specifically. Almost unconsciously, he stepped towards it.

Watson wined, trying to pull away.

Graham tugged the lead with both hands, forcing the dog to

follow.

"Who's ringing at this time?" Graham asked the cold night air.

Watson's paws dragged against the stones, trying to twist away. Deep in the back of its throat, the dog let out primal, guttural squeals. It wasn't some subtle change in temperature or magnetism that had spooked the dog. It wasn't the scent of predators downwind. As the dog's startled eyes glimpsed the looming telephone box, eyes that had only ever glimpsed the world in black and white now saw a third colour. Blood red.

The piercing ringing was so loud in Graham's ears it was almost deafening. Hands that were tempted to clamp over his ears instead reached out to grasp the handle of the box.

"Why is it so bloody loud?" Graham shouted, barely hearing his own voice.

Watson dropped to his belly, dragged along the stones. Writhing against his lead, teeth bared, tail between his legs.

To the dog's ears, there was no sound at all. There never had been.

Just the wind.

# Chapter One

The cafe's 'closed' sign had barely swivelled to 'open' when Agent Radford pushed on the door. The sight of his hand emerging from the darkness to slap on the glass must have been quite alarming for the young waitress, who jumped a mile, sign still clutched between her fingers. She recovered well, hand clasped to her chest and elevated breathing the only indication that she'd momentarily feared for her life. Agent Radford and Junior-Agent Stone walked inside, the little brass bell above the door jangling happily at the sight of new customers.

"You chaps must be hungry!" The waitress had a sweet voice, smothered in Yorkshire twang, "Don't normally get anyone in 'til half past."

"This lad's always hungry," said Agent Radford, thumbing over his shoulder at his younger colleague. "And we've got a busy day on, you see." He raised the newspaper rolled up in his hand and gave her the type of grandfatherly wink that only men of a certain age can get away with.

Both men were nothing to look at. In fact, if you were to look, your eyes might slide right over them, the same way you don't examine individual bricks in a wall. They were extraordinarily ordinary. Much like anyone in Yorkshire who plans on surviving the winter, they wore large coats above their work shirts and trousers. Radford's was trailing and dark grey, Stone's was brown and only fell to his belt. Both had lots of clever little pockets that if you cared to look - which again, you wouldn't - bulged with mysterious lumps.

"Sit anywhere you like except the table at the back there," said the waitress, pointing to a solitary table and chair shoved up into the corner of the cafe, "that one's reserved."

The two men picked a table near the kitchen, Radford uncurling his newspaper and Stone grabbing the menu. Radford had already read the headlines earlier. That was, of course, why they were here. Management had spotted a pattern, and Management was never wrong when it came to patterns.

The newspaper itself was very dull, and today's stories were mundane enough to put even the most avid gossip to sleep. Flicking through to the puzzle section, Radford plucked a pencil stowed above his ear and scrawled an answer to a half-completed crossword. Seven down. The clue said "When you get there", but Radford didn't even read it.

'ARRIVED', he wrote.

At the sound of footsteps, he thoughtfully tapped the pencil against his lips, his face a studious picture of concentration.

"Anything to drink?" asked the waitress.

"Tea please," said both men in unison.

"And to eat?"

"Large breakfast please, love," said Stone, "No mushrooms."

Radford slid the menu across the table and gave it a brief consideration. "I'll just have a small."

The waitress nodded, quickly jotting down their order and disappearing into the kitchen. Radford looked down at his crossword, where some extra answers had decided to appear all by themselves.

'MALE' said one.

'BLACK HAIR' said another.

One answer simply read '6:30AM'

"That's good," said Radford, looking up from his newspaper. "We'll have enough time to finish our breakfast before he shows."

"Uhuh," muttered Stone. The young man was gazing down at his own forearm, glancing occasionally up at the kitchen to ensure he wasn't being watched. His sleeve was rolled up, and just between his elbow and wrist was an intricate tattoo of an hourglass. With a pen clutched in his free hand, Junior-Agent Stone drew a dashed line across the sand mark of his tattoo.

"You rely on that thing too much," said Radford, shaking his head and rubbing out the answers to his crossword. Only the ones he'd written himself rubbed out; those that had appeared of their own accord weren't written in pencil, but took the hint and vanished much the same way they'd arrived.

"Might save my life one day," said Stone, recapping his pen and stowing it back inside his shirt pocket. Blowing on the fresh ink, he tested it was dry before buttoning up his shirt sleeve. "Figure my life's worth saving. I wouldn't get much done without it."

Radford flicked a sugar packet at his young colleague, who didn't notice until it collided with his chest. "Might be the reason you snuff it. So busy staring down at that tattoo, you miss what's happening in front of you."

Stone rolled his eyes. "I'm not worried about rogue condiments."

"How about being paralysed? Or poisoned? Or knocked unconscious?" asked Radford, emphasising each point with a flick of an additional sugar packet. As the kitchen door swung open, he stretched back in his chair and kept his tone conversational, barely above a murmur. "None of those would show up on your little tattoo..."

Approaching footsteps pressed both men to silence. Radford turned his newspaper over to the sports page, and Stone gained a sudden fascination with the menu. The waitress placed two steaming mugs of tea on the table.

"Cheers."

"Cheers, love."

As the kitchen doors swung shut again, the men resumed their conversation, voices never drifting beyond their own table.

"If you want to get to my ripe old age," said Radford, wry smile twisting his grey moustache, "you need to learn to trust your gut."

Stone snatched up his mug. "I think I'd rather be poisoned..." he muttered, taking a cautious first sip and wincing as the tea scalded his lips.

Permitting himself a small smile, Radford wondered if he'd ever seen Stone consume a hot drink without burning his mouth first. "Each time you survive on your own wits, your wits get a little stronger. But when you let your tools become a crutch, you get lazy. And your wits turn into mush. Besides..." Radford rolled up his sleeve and revealed his own tattoo - identical to Stone's except for the amount of sand, "when you're as close to the bottom as I am, it's hard to use the bloody thing for anything other than certain death."

Stone did his best to appear casual as he leaned forwards and tilted his head, trying to count the grains of the tattoo, trying to work out how much of Radford's life was left.

"Oh, stop it," hissed Radford, snatching his arm back and fastening up his sleeve. "Point is, if I'd relied on it all my life, I'd be buggered now, wouldn't I? Tools are useful, but if you always need them - if you can't cope without them - you're in trouble."

Stone was silent for a moment, tapping a finger against his lips as he formed his retort. "Bullshit," he said finally, pointing a lecturing finger across the table. "If someone gives me a hammer, why would I keep knocking nails in with my fist? It hurts, it doesn't work, and I've got a hammer now."

Half sighing, half blowing on his tea, Radford shook his head. "It's not the same. You need to respect your gut, that's all I'm saying. It's just like any other muscle. The more you use it, the stronger it gets. You were already given the right tools for the job when you were born. That thing is a luxury, and using it too much just makes you paranoid."

The double doors of the kitchen flew open, and flapped together again as dainty footsteps approached their table. Stone eased up, leaning back in his chair, hands patting his belly. "Speaking of respecting your gut..."

"Large breakfast?" asked the waitress.

"Please," said Stone, maneuvering a salt shaker and his mug of tea to make space for the plate.

Radford could smell it now. Sausage, bacon, mushrooms. Fat and grease, wafting over from the kitchen. Cheap perfume, as the waitress leant over to place his plate down.

"And a small," she said.

"Ta."

"Cheers, love," said Stone, already stuffing a slice of toast into his mouth. He ate his meals the same way he drank his tea.

Radford decided he best tuck in himself, before Stone finished his breakfast and started looking for more. The junior agent was prodding at his food with a fork as he ate, counting each item and searching for any hidden hash browns.

"Wasn't worth the extra two quid, was it?" said Radford, without looking up.

Pausing halfway through slicing his egg open, Stone pointed his knife accusingly across the table. "Stop doing that," he said, yolk dripping onto the table.

"Stop doing what?" asked Radford.

Stone let the knife point linger, before taking his frustration out on a sausage. "Telling me what I'm thinking..."

Radford dabbed at his mouth with a napkin, then - knowing exactly how much it would irritate his younger colleague - wiped away Stone's yolk stain from the table. "Stop showing me then."

Stone muttered something between mouthfuls, but it was too quiet to catch. Something about 'not my mother'.

The way Stone ate, anyone would think it was a competition. If it was, he won, and from the way he eyed Radford's remaining breakfast, anyone would think he expected that to be his prize. Radford slowly dragged a crust of toast around his plate, mopping up bean juice. Finally, he nodded at his final slice and said "have it if you want."

The words weren't even out of Radford's mouth before the toast was in Stone's. He practically inhaled it. "See," began Stone, reclining in his seat, patting his stomach like a pet dog, "your gut is just like any other muscle in your body. The more you use-"

"Oh, shush."

The front door of the cafe opened, threshold scratching across the bristles of the doormat. High above, the bell jangled merrily enough, announcing another customer. Neither Radford or Stone looked up as heavy black boots took several steps inside, then froze.

"Might as well sit down, Marco," Radford told the air. He met Stone's eyes and nodded towards the kitchen door. Stone necked the last of his tea and rose out of his seat, stepping towards the kitchen.

There was a long reluctant pause as Marco hovered in the doorway, considering his choices.

"Don't you dare run," Radford said sternly, turning in his chair to glare at the man. "You'll only give me stitch and a temper."

Marco pursed his lips and eventually stepped towards Radford, pulling out a chair and sitting at the table next to him. He was a slither of a man, in his later years. What was left of his hair was retreating backwards and greying, and he peered nervously through tinted glasses that magnified his frantic eyes.

"Good morning, Agent," said Marco, much the same way you might say 'good morning' to a snake on your pillow.

"Is it?" asked Radford, watching Marco over the rim of his cup as he sipped his tea.

Marco shifted in his seat. He licked his lips, clearly forming sentences in his mind but never letting them leave his tongue. Hard to believe someone over two-hundred years old could be this unsure of himself.

"Hungry?" asked Radford, setting down his cup. "I'm sure if we asked they'd give you some black pudding."

"I'm fine," muttered Marco, fixing the ground with a hard stare.

"Already eaten, have you?"

Marco sneered through his nose, an insincere smile plastered across his face. "Whatever you think I've done," he whispered, leaning forwards, "you're wrong."

Radford nodded slowly. “Maybe,” he admitted. There was a heavy thunk as Agent Radford placed a revolver on the cafe table, finger resting on the trigger, barrel pointing at Marco’s chest. “Or, maybe you save us both some time and tell me what you were doing last night.”

Marco’s shoulders slumped inwards, head bowing. “I haven’t done anything wrong, Agent,” he groaned, shaking his head, “please don’t take me back to Thirty.”

Radford said nothing. He didn’t need to now. The revolver was singing its silent song and soon Marco would be dancing to the tune.

“Look,” Marco sighed, rubbing at his eyes, “look. I haven’t got anything to do with that missing man.”

“Men,” corrected Radford.

Marco’s eyes went wide at that. The reaction seemed genuine, but Radford didn’t allow himself to soften. Not yet.

“There’s been another?” whispered Marco.

Radford nodded. “Last night. You’re the only registered Parahuman we have in the surrounding area, so... would you like to tell me why you broke curfew?”

"It wasn't..." began Marco, fumbling around for words to grasp. "I just went for a walk."

"A walk," said Radford flatly, taking another sip of tea as he watched Marco with unblinking eyes.

"Just a walk," replied Marco hoarsely.

Agent Radford watched him for a moment in between slow, measured drinks that were more for show than taste. Marco flinched as the revolver was dragged away and disappeared into the depths of Radford's jacket. "Let's get your coffee then. We'll take it to go, since you like walking so much."

Radford rose, but Marco remained in his seat, staring down

at his boots. He was so slumped, it looked like someone had doubled his gravity. Agent Stone stood at the kitchen door, keeping it propped open. One hand was stuffed into his pocket, but the way he held himself squealed that he was clutching his revolver.

"Well?" hissed Stone under his breath.

"No point whispering," replied Radford bluntly. He thumbed over his shoulder at Marco. "His hearing is too good. We'll flesh these out and get going."

Both Agents looked through the door at the waitress and cook inside the kitchen, both ashen grey and still as statues. Both staring back at the Agents with stunned expressions. Both turned to stone.

“Let’s have her behind the counter, and put him near the fridge,” said Radford, as the two Agents walked inside to assess the situation. “And put that away.”

Sheepishly, Stone raised his revolver. On the verge of tucking it away, he hesitated, and examined his hour-glass tattoo. Apparently satisfied, he stowed the weapon. “What about him?” asked Stone, gesturing conspiratorially back into the cafe.

“He’s not going anywhere, are you Marco?”

There was a short pause before a particularly bitter voice from the cafe said “No, Sir,” loud enough for the two agents to hear.

“How can you be sure?” Stone was lingering at the door, unwilling to stray too far from their lead suspect.

“Because he knows I believe him,” said Radford, loud enough for even human ears in the cafe to hear. “And he also knows if he runs, I’ll change my mind. Do us a favour and turn the lights out will you Marco? And watch for civs.”

Stone reluctantly joined his superior at the statuesque waitress, and together they each grabbed hold of her and lifted. Completely rigid and frozen in position, she was more an object than a person. Despite much grunting and straining, they barely got her off the floor.

"Christ, how long did you dose them for?" puffed Radford, lowering the stone waitress back down and stretching his shoulders. "Almost put my back out."

"Five seconds," said Stone, hand instinctively patting the thick book in his coat pocket.

"Must have been a long bloody five seconds."

A quick search of the kitchen found what Radford was looking for. A little two wheeled trolley for lifting boxes. He wheeled it over to the waitress and Stone nodded approvingly. The junior agent carefully heaved and tilted the waitress towards him, and Radford slid the metal bottom of the trolley under her shoes. Both men then carefully transported the stone waitress through the kitchen, into the near-dark of the cafe. Marco watched with a mixture of curiosity and fear as the two agents unloaded their human cargo behind the counter and returned to the kitchen.

After moving the cook over to the counter, Radford took a hip flask from his inside pocket and unscrewed the cap. He placed it to the grey stone lips of the man, and lifted it slowly, until a single purple drop of liquid spilled into his open mouth.

Next, he took out a small bottle of perfume and sprayed the cook with one quick burst in the centre of his chest. Colour bled from the grey patch where the spray hit, the apron returning to a stripey blue, patches of yellow grease and egg yolk slowly revealing themselves. Radford passed both hip flask and perfume bottle to Stone.

"There's got to be an easier way to do this," said Stone.

“If you’ve got one, I’m all ears,” muttered Radford, fetching two cartons of eggs and placing them on the counter in front of the cook. Stone disappeared to reanimate the waitress and Radford waited until the colour returned to the cook’s entire body before attempting to manoeuver his limbs into position, always with minimal force. These things weren’t to be rushed. It wasn’t brittle enough to shatter, but until flesh became flesh again, it wasn’t malleable enough to twist outright without risk of injury and bruising. Since the entire purpose of turning civilians to stone was to protect them and prevent witnesses, leaving any kind of trace or harm would be counter-productive.

“Five seconds my arse,” muttered Radford, waiting until he could move the man’s chin simply by using two fingers and the slightest amount of pressure. He guided him to look at the counter, raised both of the cook’s hands and placed an egg inside each open palm, encasing the fingers around them. The man’s flesh was starting to feel warm now. Without the milk-of-amnesia from Radford’s hip flask, the cook might be vaguely aware of his surroundings by now. As it was, he wouldn’t remember any of this, or the next couple of minutes. His mind would glue itself back together, and he’d find himself in the middle of a simple task, without remembering what he was doing or how he got there. Simplicity was key. It had to be something the mind could readily dismiss and forget about. Radford gave a quick sweep of the kitchen to ensure nothing had been missed, then returned to the cafe.

The lights were back on, and Stone was carefully adjusting the waitresses head, tweaking her to look down at the notepad she’d jotted down their original order on. She was back to her usual colour now, and had started blinking again. After a pen was placed in her hand, the three men moved to the customer side of the register.

Radford pocketed the flask and spray bottle. "If that was five seconds then Marco's a vegetarian."

"I counted properly."

"Show me."

"One potato... two potato..."

"You're pausing too long between potatoes. It's more like one potato, two potato, three-"

"I know how to count."

"One of these days I'm gonna time you. Pay up anyway, the lady's waiting."

Stone and Radford both turned to look expectantly at the waitress, whose glazed eyes slid into focus. She looked at Stone's outstretched hand, passing her a ten pound note.

"Sorry chuck," said the waitress, taking the money and opening the cash register, "I was miles away." She totted up the total, cursing herself for being so slow at the maths, before handing Stone his change.

"Oh," said Radford, "and a coffee for our friend here."

He gestured to Marco, who forced a smile.

"Morning Mark," said the waitress cheerily. "Didn't see you come in. Just the usual?"

"Morning Debra," said Marco. "Yes please."

"You fellers must have a lot on to beat Mark to breakfast," chuckled Debra as she moved to the coffee pot. "He's always my first customer normally."

"Is he now?" mused Radford, locking eyes with Marco. "Well, we're early birds too. And you know what they say about early birds..."

"Catch the worm," replied the waitress with a smile, passing the polystyrene cup to Marco, who looked like he'd swallowed a frog.

"Cheers, love," said Stone, paying for the coffee.

Radford picked up a pair of plastic milk pods. He placed them into the vampire's hands. "Two Milks, no sugar, isn't it Marco?"

The pale, gaunt man looked even paler and even gaunter as the two Agents ushered him out of the cafe. The jangling bell announced their goodbye as the waitress moved to clean up their plates.

From the kitchen, a slightly confused voice shouted "do we need eggs?"

# Don’t Forget!

I hope you’ve enjoyed this book!

If you have, please don’t forget to leave a review or rating.

Not only does this let me know you’ve enjoyed my stories, it lets other people know too! Which means they are more likely to take a chance on an unknown name.

And that means I can keep writing new stories! It really is the best way you can support new and emerging authors like me.

Thanks for reading.
Ryan Hunt

# About the Author

*Ryan Hunt was born in the gutter and raised by wolves. A freak accident involving harps helped him discover a love for music and danger. He is a certified rascal and is often suspected of telling fibs on his author bios.*

*His billions of adoring fans have eventually deduced his true identity - an Engineer from Derbyshire, England. When he's not openly lying to the general public, he can be found with a pint in his hand, and his Border Collie, Pepper, at his side.*

**You can connect with me on:**

**FloorFiftyFour.co.uk**

**Facebook - @FloorFiftyFourOfficial**

**Twitter - @FloorFiftyFour**

**Don't forget to subscribe to the Floor Fifty-Four newsletter. This way you'll always know when I have something new released into the wild!**

Printed in Great Britain
by Amazon

10846455R00124